She was too stunning for words.

Her flame-red hair was wild about her shoulders. The new do made her normally pale skin glow and look more beautiful than he'd ever imagined. And her glistening lips were…overwhelmingly kissable.

His mouth went dry at the thought. His gaze seemed to have a mind of its own as it roved down the length of her, over the curve of her tiny waist that flowed right on down into flared hips.

An hourglass. She was a soft, luscious hourglass.

He choked as the startling thought lodged in his throat like some inhaled morsel of food.

Immediately, Rachel was clapping him on the back. "You okay?" she asked.

He was trying to flee. From what, he had no clue. He worked with her in the office every single weekday. But she'd never had *this* kind of effect on him before.…

Dear Reader,

This holiday season, as our anniversary year draws to a close, we have much to celebrate. The talented authors who have published—and continue to publish—unforgettable love stories. You, the readers, who have made our twenty-year milestone possible. And this month's very special offerings.

First stop: BACHELOR GULCH, Sandra Steffen's popular ongoing miniseries. They'd shared an amazing night together; now a beguiling stranger was back in his life carrying *Sky's Pride and Joy*. She'd dreamed *Hunter's Vow* would be the marrying kind…until he learned about their child he'd never known existed—don't miss this keeper by Susan Meier! Carolyn Zane's BRUBAKER BRIDES are back! *Montana's Feisty Cowgirl* thought she could pass as just another *male* ranch hand, but Montana wouldn't rest till he knew her secrets…and made this 100% woman completely his!

Donna Clayton's SINGLE DOCTOR DADS return…STAT. *Rachel and the M.D.* were office assistant and employer…so why was she imagining herself this widower's bride and his triplets' mother? Diana Whitney brings her adorable STORK EXPRESS series from Special Edition into Romance with the delightful story of what happens when *Mixing Business…with Baby*. And debut author Belinda Barnes tells the charming tale of a jilted groom who finds himself all dressed up…to deliver a pregnant beauty's baby—don't miss *His Special Delivery!*

Thank you for celebrating our 20th anniversary. In 2001 we'll have even more excitement—the return of ROYALLY WED and Marie Ferrarella's 100th book, to name a couple!

Happy reading!

Mary-Theresa Hussey

Mary-Theresa Hussey
Senior Editor

Please address questions and book requests to:
Silhouette Reader Service
U.S.: 3010 Walden Ave., P.O. Box 1325, Buffalo, NY 14269
Canadian: P.O. Box 609, Fort Erie, Ont. L2A 5X3

Rachel and the M.D.

DONNA CLAYTON

SILHOUETTE *Romance*®

Published by Silhouette Books

America's Publisher of Contemporary Romance

This book is dedicated, in loving memory, to
Louise Anderson

SILHOUETTE BOOKS

ISBN 0-373-19489-7

RACHEL AND THE M.D.

Copyright © 2000 by Donna Fasano

All rights reserved. Except for use in any review, the reproduction
or utilization of this work in whole or in part in any form by any
electronic, mechanical or other means, now known or hereafter
invented, including xerography, photocopying and recording, or in
any information storage or retrieval system, is forbidden without
the written permission of the editorial office, Silhouette Books,
300 East 42nd Street, New York, NY 10017 U.S.A.

All characters in this book have no existence outside the imagination of
the author and have no relation whatsoever to anyone bearing the same
name or names. They are not even distantly inspired by any individual
known or unknown to the author, and all incidents are pure invention.

This edition published by arrangement with Harlequin Books S.A.

® and TM are trademarks of Harlequin Books S.A., used under license.
Trademarks indicated with ® are registered in the United States Patent
and Trademark Office, the Canadian Trade Marks Office and in other
countries.

Visit Silhouette at www.eHarlequin.com

Printed in U.S.A.

Books by Donna Clayton

Silhouette Romance

Mountain Laurel #720
Taking Love in Stride #781
Return of the Runaway Bride #999
Wife for a While #1039
Nanny and the Professor #1066
Fortune's Bride #1118
Daddy Down the Aisle #1162
*Miss Maxwell Becomes a Mom #1211
*Nanny in the Nick of Time #1217
*Beauty and the Bachelor Dad #1223
†The Stand-By Significant Other #1284
†Who's the Father of Jenny's Baby? #1302
The Boss and the Beauty #1342
His Ten-Year-Old Secret #1373
Her Dream Come True #1399
Adopted Dad #1417
His Wild Young Bride #1441
**The Nanny Proposal #1477
**The Doctor's Medicine Woman #1483
**Rachel and the M.D. #1489

*The Single Daddy Club
†Mother & Child
**Single Doctor Dads

DONNA CLAYTON

is proud to be a recipient of the Holt Medallion, an award honoring outstanding literary talent, for her Silhouette Romance novel *Wife for a While*. And seeing her work appear on the Waldenbooks Series Bestsellers list has given her a great deal of joy and satisfaction.

Reading is one of Donna's favorite ways to wile away a rainy afternoon. She loves to hike, too. Another hobby added to her list of fun things to do is traveling. She fell in love with Europe during her first trip abroad and plans to return often. Oh, and Donna still collects cookbooks, but as her writing career grows, she finds herself using them less and less.

Donna loves to hear from her readers. Please write to her care of Silhouette Books, 300 East 42nd Street, New York, NY 10017.

Sloan Radcliff, M.D.
Family Practice
Philadelphia, Pennsylvania

Patient File

Name: <u>Me</u>

Diagnosis: <u>Struggling to raise three adolescent daughters—alone.</u>

Symptoms: <u>Exhausted, overwhelmed...love starved.</u>

Prescription: <u>Find a beautiful woman who will nurture the girls and</u>
<u>soothe my soul...stat!</u>

Sloan Radcliff
Physician's Signature

Chapter One

There's a look that narrows the eyes of a nearly teen adolescent—a look reflecting stubbornness-bordering-on-rebellion—that strikes terror in the heart of any normal parent. And Sloan Radcliff was receiving that very look from not one, but *three* pairs of eyes. The defiant expressions he confronted belonged to his daughters, his twelve-year-old triplet terrors.

Sloan tamped down the myriad of emotions creating chaos in his head and focused on keeping his voice calm, his nerves steely.

"Girls," he quietly began. The experience of being a single parent for the last two years had taught him that, when dealing with his children's obstinacy, a tranquil tone never really helped very much. However, he *was* the mature, sane adult here and he did want to act in a manner befitting that fact. For as long as he could possibly hold out, anyway.

"You know the rules," he continued. "Nine o'clock. That's curfew. You're twelve years old. It's not an unreasonable request."

"Sez who?"

Oh, Lord. Sydney, the most quick-tempered of his three daughters, was already becoming bluntly outspoken. He chose to ignore the fact that her short question was laced around the edges with insolence.

"Daddy," Sasha whined pitifully, "this is going to be the party *of the year.* All the coolest kids will be there. We *have* to go. We just *have to.* If we don't, we'll be labeled as *geeks."* Her eyes were wide, her forehead furrowed, her arms gesturing wildly. All indications that if this classification were to take place, her entire existence would be ruined for all eternity.

Sloan's brows rose a fraction. Not because Sasha was being overly dramatic—that was her trademark—but it was awfully early in the dispute for her to start displaying her well-oiled thespian skills. This New Year's Eve get-together must be more important to his daughters than he'd first realized.

Glancing over at Sophie, the third of his lovely, lively daughters, he wasn't surprised to see her arms crossed tightly over her rib cage, her mouth pressed together in a firm line.

With their long, straight brown hair and their nut-brown eyes, his girls might look like peas in a pod, but their characters—the methods they used to cope with everything from joy and success to anger, disappointment and stress—were as different as the snowflakes that now fell from the wintry, late December sky.

"Look, Dad," Sydney piped up, "we've been asking you about this party for a month. Now it's time to go shopping for dresses and shoes and stuff. We're down to the wire. We need an answer. Now.''

"Shopping?" he asked. "But all three of you just received new clothes for Christmas—"

Sasha's wide-eyed look of horror cut his protest off in midstream.

"You can't expect us to wear those things," Sasha said. "We got jeans and sweaters. Knock-around clothes. We need *gowns.*"

"Yes," Sydney agreed with her sister. "We need long, elegant dresses. Everyone there will be wearing them."

Seeing a means of lightening the mood, Sloan allowed exaggerated skepticism to tug at one corner of his mouth as he teased, "The boys are going to look pretty silly in—"

"*Dad,*" both Sydney and Sasha chimed. They shook their head in disgust.

"Our *girl*friends," Sydney supplied. "You knew what we meant."

"We need an answer," Sasha pressed him. "The party is just four days away. Are you gonna let us go?"

He'd put off his girls as long as he could. He needed to make a decision. Let them go to the party? Or protect them, and at the same time, disappoint them terribly?

During times like this, he really hated being a single dad. With both sets of his daughters' grandparents deceased, and him with no siblings, Sloan had no one to talk these things over with. He felt... lonely. Lost. And terribly unsure. He never knew for certain whether or not he was making the right choice. He needed more time.

"Girls, you can't just come traipsing into my office, demanding—"

"All your patients are gone, Dad," Sydney said. "The waiting room is empty."

"It's time for you to go home." Sasha plunked her hand on her hip. "Besides, you were expecting us. Remember? You asked Annie's mom to drop us off here."

Of course Sloan remembered the girls had spent the day with a friend. He'd just been hedging for time.

"Sure, I remember," he said jovially. He stood and pulled off his white lab coat. "How about if we stop off on the way home and pick up some burgers and fries for dinner? We'll go to your favorite place."

Three pairs of eyes glowered at him.

"We won't let you change the subject, Dad." Now Sydney, too, had her hands on her hips, her elbows cocked at wide angles.

"We want to go to the party!" Sasha said.

Sophie only nodded tightly, her gaze silently reflecting all the anxiety she was feeling.

Sloan sighed. He felt damned tired. He sat down, rubbed his palms up and down his thighs.

"Okay," he said, "you can go to the party—"

"Whooo-hoo," Sydney shouted.

"Yes!" Sasha threw her hands into the air and performed a joyful little jig.

Even Sophie smiled, the tension in her shoulders visibly melting away.

The girls began chattering to one another all at once.

"I'm going to get that black strapless dress I saw in the mall—"

"I'm wearing that electric-blue one with the slits up both sides—"

"I need panty hose and I want those strappy platform sandals—"

"And let's not forget to go to the drugstore for makeup. I saw a tube of red lipstick I've just gotta have—"

Strapless dress? Electric-blue slits? Panty hose? Platform sandals? Red lipstick?

Sloan didn't think so. Not while he still had breath in his body.

"Hold it!"

His daughters turned to face him, their excitement suddenly dimmed by his rare show of anger.

"I wasn't finished," he continued, not bothering to remove the edginess from his tone. "You can go to the party. But you can't stay out until two o'clock in the morning."

"But, *Dad*—" Sasha lamented.

"Oh, no—" the two little words Sydney emitted sounded like a groan from a horribly wounded animal "—he's going to embarrass us. He's going to ruin everything. Everyone will be looking at us. He's going to make us leave early."

She made the idea of premature departure sound like some sort of disfiguring disease. He wanted to point out just what kind of attention twelve-year-olds wearing revealing dresses and red lipstick would attract, but he chomped down firmly on his tongue and kept the thoughts to himself.

Sophie quietly pointed out. "Dad, Debbie's mother rented a hall."

Sloan shrugged. "I don't care if Debbie's mother rented Veterans' Stadium. My daughters will not be out until the wee hours of the morning. You girls are twelve years old—"

Sydney's chin rose, as did her voice, when she pointed out, "But I'll be thirteen in three weeks."

"Me, too," Sasha said.

Through her tight jaw, Sophie added, "Me, three."

This was their motto. Their united credo.

Rebellion glinted in their gazes now, bold and unmistakable.

Holding his ground, Sloan refused to be intimidated. "I don't care if you're going to be thirty-five. No daughter of mine is going to be out gallivanting in the middle of the night. You can celebrate the New Year, and I'll be picking you up at twelve-thirty. And that's final."

Sasha's bottom lip began to tremble, piteous tears welling in her big brown eyes.

"But Debbie's mom is serving breakfast at one," Sydney informed him. "And she's making my favorite. Pancakes."

"I'll be happy to make pancakes just as soon as we get home from the party," Sloan offered. But his words were firm, uncontestable.

The air grew tense and thick, and Sloan got the strange sense that something awful was about to happen.

Fate didn't disappoint him.

Sophie—the quietest of his daughters—straightened her spine and squared her shoulders. She looked her father directly in the eye and proclaimed, ''Well, I'm staying until the end of the party. I'm not going to let you ruin my first date with Bobby Snyders.''

Date? Had his little girl just said she had a date? With a *boy?*

Rachel Richards loved her job. She managed the medical practice of partners Sloan Radcliff, Travis Westcott and Greg Hamilton. The three men were more than doctors sharing a practice, they were friends who supported one another. Since she had no close relatives to speak of, the family-like atmosphere of the office was one of the reasons she so liked working there.

There were other reasons as well. Sloan and his daughters made up a big part of those reasons.

The seemingly never-ending pile of patient insurance forms had been a convenient excuse for her to remain at the office after hours, but the truth was she knew the triplets had planned to confront their father today about the party and she wanted to be nearby…just in case.

She'd loved those girls ever since her best friend Olivia, Sloan's wife, had given birth to them. And Rachel had done everything she could to nurture them during the two years since Olivia had passed away.

The triplets shouldn't gang up on their father the way they were doing this afternoon. Rachel had seen a lot of that kind of behavior lately. The girls acted like a pack of wild dogs, nipping and yelping from all sides, until Sloan caved in to their demands. And it seemed that, as the girls got older, the more crafty they became. Today they were showing just how they had perfected this "pack hunting" technique.

Rachel had remained at the office in order to dry their tears and smooth their ruffled feathers should Sloan refuse to allow them to attend the New Year's Eve party. But as soon as she overheard the word *date,* she knew it was Sloan who was in urgent need of her support.

And if there was anything she could do for Sloan... Her heart raced. Anything at all...

With insurance papers still in one hand, a pen in the other, Rachel hurried into Sloan's office.

His handsome face was ghostly pale when she entered the room. And his sensual mouth—the one that so often intruded on her dreams in the deepest, most vulnerable part of the night—was gaping as he so obviously searched for something to say.

Empathy for his plight welled up inside Rachel. She knew he agonized over his parenting responsibilities. Not that he bent her ear or leaned on her shoulder—she only wished he would. However, she knew he relied heavily on his friends and partners, Greg Hamilton and Travis Westcott.

Being a single, childless woman, Rachel really hadn't a clue how to fix this problem between Sloan and his daughters. But she had to try. She simply had to.

Plastering a bright smile onto her face, she rustled up her courage and said, "Sounds like a little compromise is in order here."

Four pairs of eyes turned to look at her. Focusing on Sloan's chocolate-brown ones would be a mistake, she knew. Her tongue would tie up in knots. So she directed her attention to the girls, letting her gaze bounce from one to the next.

"It's clear that your dad wants to let you go to the party," she told them. "I overheard him say as much. But all three of you are going to have to be willing to make a few concessions where wardrobe and...and...a few other things are concerned."

"Kids are always the ones who have to make concessions," Sydney muttered.

"Well," Rachel said smoothly, "nobody ever said that life is fair."

After only a second or two, Rachel continued, "That party invitation you showed me stated that this shindig is semiformal."

"Yes." Sasha's eyes brightened, evidently seeing Rachel as some sort of co-conspirator who had arrived to save the day. "That's what we *tried* to explain to Dad. That we'd all need long gowns."

"Honey, I hate to break this to you—" Rachel's head tilted gently "—but semiformal does not mean fancy evening dresses."

"Doesn't mean strapless gowns or electric-blue slits, either," Sloan murmured under his breath.

Rachel suppressed the small smile tugging at her mouth, but the obvious appreciation she read in his brown gaze made her breath hitch in her throat.

"How about," she offered, forcing herself to focus on the girls once again, "if I take the three of you shopping? We'll buy nice, tasteful dresses that your father will approve of."

"B-but all the girls are wearing—"

"Trust me on this, Sydney," Rachel said firmly.

"What about makeup?" Sasha looked sulky, her bottom lip protruding.

Rachel reached out and touched the girl's cheek with her fingertips. "You're so beautiful you don't need makeup. But maybe your dad will agree to a little lightly tinted lip gloss. That'll accentuate your cute mouth without too much garish color. What do you say, Sloan?"

Again, the gratitude in his intense eyes made her feel as if all the air in the room had condensed. He smiled at her. Blood thrummed through her body.

And then that familiar guilt descended on her like a thick, heavy layer of wet wool. It congealed in her chest and she fought to swallow a nervous cough.

"I think I could live with that." Sloan nodded, evidently not noticing the chaos coursing through her.

Sophie stepped toward Rachel. "But what about having to leave the party early? We can't—"

"Don't push it, Sophie," Rachel softly warned, narrowing her eyes in a manner that conveyed the same gentle but firm message. "We don't even know if that's negotiable. We'll let your dad think about it. Then he can let you know."

She addressed all three girls, "Go get into your coats. I'll meet you in the waiting area."

Once the two of them were alone, Sloan said, "I really appreciate this, Rachel."

The richness of his voice nearly made her toes curl with pleasure.

"Oh, it's nothing," she told him. Had someone

been fiddling with the thermostat? she wondered. It sure was hot in this office. "I'm happy to take the girls to the mall."

He pulled out his wallet and handed her some money. "This is for dinner. That band of raving rebels will be hungry before long." Affection candy-coated his words. Then he paused, sudden indecision shadowing his gaze. "Should I be going along with you?"

"Nah." A tiny smile twisted one corner of her mouth. "We'll probably end up shopping at half a dozen different stores before we're through. It would be very boring for you."

"Well, put the dresses on your charge account and I'll pay the bill when it arrives."

She nodded. "Fair enough." This part was routine. She'd taken the girls shopping for clothing many times. Then she told him, "I'll have them home before nine."

"Drive safe," he said, glancing out the window. "The snow has thinned, but it's still coming down out there."

Rachel would have loved to think his words of warning were because he was worried about her safety. But she knew his daughters were the precious cargo at the forefront of his mind, as they should be.

"The roads have been salted."

However, before the words had even left her mouth, Sloan had already turned his attention to the patient file sitting open on his desk. So she left his office and strolled down the hallway toward the sounds of the girls' excited chatter.

She really was happy to have the opportunity to

help Sloan and his daughters. Terribly happy. She just wished she would stop being engulfed by this wave of tremendous guilt—a wave that threatened to drown her each and every time she and Sloan were together.

Oh, she knew what caused this awful, dark emotion. Knew it just as well as she knew her own name.

The guilt was her conscience. An inner voice that constantly told her she had no right—no right, whatsoever—to have fallen in love with her best friend's husband.

"Rachel, can I ask you a question?"

The snow blanketing the city wasn't all that thick, but it was substantial enough to muffle the city sounds from outside. And the interior of the car seemed quieter, too.

"Sure, Sophie." Rachel glanced into the rearview mirror, but couldn't make out the child's face. "Ask me anything."

"Well...w-what..." Sophie paused, then tried again. "What does it feel like...you know...to kiss a boy?"

Rachel's brows rose. She'd fully expected to hear complaints about Sloan's stubbornness, about what the girls surely labeled their father's overprotective nature. It hadn't dawned on her that Sophie's question would deal with relationships. Wow, this conversation just might lead to a discussion about the birds and the bees.

However, rather than being distressed by the prospect, Rachel felt honored. Sophie's question let Rachel know the girls felt comfortable with her. Comfortable to talk about anything. Even kissing boys.

Before she could answer, Sydney giggled at her sister's query. But Sasha's tone was awestruck as she asked Sophie, "Do you really think Bobby will kiss you at the party?"

Rachel sensed Sophie's shrug.

"Well, it's New Year's Eve," Sophie began slowly. "People always hug and kiss to celebrate the coming in of the new year, right?"

Sasha's voice became even more breathless. "You're right. They do."

Sydney's laughter quickly died, and she, too, seemed overwhelmed by the prospect that her sister might experience her first real, honest-to-goodness kiss in just four short days.

The air felt all shivery with apprehension.

"There's nothing to be nervous about," Rachel said softly. "It's nice. Being kissed, I mean. When your lips touch, it'll feel…nice. Warm. But the biggest reaction you'll have is inside. Your stomach will become jumpy. Jittery. Giddy. You'll feel lightheaded, and your knees will get weak."

Where on earth was this description coming from? Rachel wondered. She hadn't been kissed in so long…she couldn't even remember how long it had been! Where did she get off telling the triplets what to expect?

"Ick!" Sydney said. "Sounds like flu symptoms to me."

Rachel didn't have time to chuckle before Sasha's serious tone cut in, "You'll have to make sure you brush your teeth, Sophie. You wouldn't want to smell like those cocktail wienies that Debbie said her mom is going to serve as snacks.''

Sydney absently played with her zipper, the metal teeth grinding as the coat was anxiously fastened and unfastened. ''And you know how Debbie's mom thinks she's a gourmet cook. She puts garlic in *everything*.''

''Gosh,'' Sophie said, ''I won't be able to eat all night.''

''Sure you will.'' Rachel pulled the car to a halt at a stop sign and looked for oncoming traffic. ''Just keep a stick of gum or a breath mint handy, and pop it into your mouth a few minutes before the countdown begins.''

Sophie's voice was tight as she declared, ''I'll just die of embarrassment if Dad makes us leave the party too early.''

Rachel sensed rather than saw the other two girls nod in silent agreement.

''Why is Dad so uptight, anyway?'' Sydney asked.

''Doesn't he know that curfews are…jeez, well, that they're so old-fashioned?'' Sasha added.

Rachel suppressed a sigh. ''He loves you,'' she told the girls. ''He's only trying to be the best dad he can be. And as for curfews being old-fashioned—'' she couldn't keep the humor out of her voice ''—I want to hear you tell me that again once you're raising children of your own.''

''Oh, I would never tell my kids when they have to come in.''

Laughter actually bubbled up from Rachel's throat, and she had trouble quelling it. She found the utter sincerity in Sydney's tone comical, although she knew the child really thought she meant what she was saying.

"And I would *never* make them leave a party early."

Sophie's sullen countenance made Rachel sigh. "Look, guys. You're going to the party. You'd better be willing to compromise about when you come home."

"We *are* going to the party," Sasha agreed with Rachel, pointing out the fact to her siblings. "And we get to pick out new dresses, too."

The parking lot of the mall was nearly deserted on this snowy night.

"I say we have some dinner," Rachel said as she turned off the engine of her car. "Then we'll hit the stores."

"Look, Rachel won't be gone for long," Sydney told her sisters in the restaurant. "She'll be back from the ladies' room before we know it…so listen up, we need to talk."

"About what?" Sasha asked, dipping a French fry in ketchup and nibbling the end. "This curfew thing?"

Sophie looked interested.

"Not just the curfew," Sydney said. "But Dad in general. He's so protective. It's weirding me out."

"Me, too," Sasha agreed.

Sophie automatically whispered, "Me, three," the onion ring she held in her fingers for the moment forgotten.

"We've gotta do something," Sydney declared.

"And we've gotta do it now. Or he's going to ruin our lives. We're going to be *teenagers* next month."

The other sisters nodded, all three growing silent as they pondered. Any passerby would have gotten the impression that the girls were contemplating paradise.

"We need to find some way to get him to stop pestering us about where we're going and who we're with and when we'll be home."

Sasha's mouth curled up derisively. "This is Dad we're talking about. That's never going to happen."

Insulted, Sydney shot back, "It could happen. All we need is a plan."

"What we need," Sophie said, "is to present Dad with something other than us to concentrate on."

"His patients have always taken up a lot of his time." Another French fry disappeared between Sasha's lips.

"It's not nice to hope people get sick." Sophie dropped the onion ring and wiped her fingers on a napkin.

"I'd never do that." Sasha looked aggrieved. "I was just sayin'—"

"What we *need*," Sydney said, "is a diversion for Dad."

"Hey!" Sophie's dark eyes lit up. "Remember when Dr. Greg hired that nanny a couple months ago? Miss Jane turned his life upside down."

"We're too old for a nanny," Sydney said.

"Jeez, Sydney, you're so infantile." Sophie rolled her eyes. "I'm not talking about a nanny for us. I'm talking about a nanny for Dad."

Her sisters looked at her as if they thought she had lost her marbles.

Again she rolled her eyes. "A *woman*...for *Dad*."

"*Eeewww!*" Sasha's face scrunched up tight. "What woman would want Dad? He's *old*."

"Wow, Sophie," Sydney breathed, "you're a genius. I remember Dr. Greg called Dad and Dr. Travis and asked them to come into the office for those emergency meetings of theirs lots of times. All about Miss Jane."

Sophie looked more sure of herself. "And come to think of it, Dr. Travis is pretty shook up over having Miss Diana came to live with him, too." She took a moment to ponder.

"How are we going to get a woman to come live with us?" Sasha was clearly baffled.

"We don't really need to have some woman in our house...do we?" Trepidation weighed heavy in Sydney's voice.

Sophie shook her head. "All we need is a distraction. Something that will take Dad's focus off us. Like Miss Jane captured Dr. Greg's attention. And Miss Diana has Dr. Travis's. We need for Dad to get all worked up. Just like Dr. Greg and Dr. Travis. We need Dad to get so upset that he'll call special meetings and stuff." Her brow furrowed suddenly. "Wonder why men can't work out their woman troubles by themselves?"

"That's what we need!" Sydney said. "Or rather, that's what Dad needs. Woman troubles."

"Okay," Sasha agreed, "but we're right back to where we were before. Where are we going to find a woman who would be the least bit interested in our father?'' Again, her face screwed up as if the mere idea was downright repulsive.

''Lots of kids at school have parents who are divorced,'' Sophie said.

Sasha blurted, ''Hey, Debbie's mom is single.''

''Don't even go there!'' Sydney shivered. ''Could you imagine Dad hooked up with Debbie's mom? That woman is too snobby for her own good.''

''I'm with you,'' Sophie said. ''I don't mind going to Debbie's party, but I don't want her to be my stepsister.''

''Jeez,'' Sasha said, anxiety lighting her eyes, ''you never said this woman-trouble thing would turn into anything permanent. I don't know...'' She was obviously having some serious second thoughts.

''Hey,'' Sophie said, ''I don't want Dad to get married...or...or even have a steady girlfriend any more than you do. But if we're going to have any fun during our teenage years, we've gotta do something!''

Sydney spoke again, ''And if there's any chance of Dad gettin' married, I sure don't want to be related to any of the kids from school. Talk about weird.''

All three were silent as they thought about their dilemma.

Finally, Sasha said, ''Well, I hate to keep bringing this up, but we still haven't solved the problem of finding a woman.''

Just then Rachel arrived back at the table.

The clear and obvious solution smacked all three of the girls in the face at the same instant. Their eyes widened as they looked at one another.

And then they burst into gales of giggles.

Rachel cocked her head to one side. "What scheme are you girls hatching now?" she asked.

The girls laughed all the harder.

"I'm so glad you saved me a few of those onion rings," Rachel said, swiping one from the plate and popping it into her mouth. Then she slid into the booth next to Sophie, like an innocent lamb strolling into a butcher's shop.

Chapter Two

Something odd was going on. The girls' behavior was…fishy. They seemed to be arguing among themselves, Rachel thought. However, their voices never rose above a hushed whisper and they seemed to engage in this secret battle only when they went into the dressing rooms to try on outfits. And every time Rachel was stirred to intervene and probe the problem, they would smile up at her innocently and make some remark that led her to believe that they were deliriously happy with their siblings and all was right with the world.

Yes, something was definitely fishy.

In the department store, Rachel had slipped into the fitting area with a lovely dress made of a fabric she thought Sydney would love. As she stood on one side of the curtain, Sophie and Sydney on the other, Rachel overheard Sophie snap, "I will *not* let you ruin my evening."

To which Sydney had replied, "But this was *your* idea!"

Rachel had no clue what Sydney had suggested that might spoil their shopping trip at the mall, and she hadn't a chance to hear another word as Sasha rushed into the fitting area behind her, loudly calling Rachel's name and proclaiming how much she adored the dress Rachel had chosen for Sydney.

Luckily, whatever hullabaloo had been brewing between the triplets eventually subsided and died away completely. Or seemed to, at least. And two and a half hours after arriving at the mall, having visited only one major department store and three apparel shops, the girls were outfitted for the party.

"These after-Christmas sales are great," Rachel said, smiling through her fatigue. "Your dad is going to be quite pleased when he learns how much money we saved."

Judging from the girls' lukewarm reactions, Rachel came to the conclusion that frugality wasn't in their adolescent dictionary.

"What do you say we stop at the food court for an ice cream before we head home?" she asked them.

Their reactions to this suggestion weren't the least bit hesitant *or* halfhearted. Rachel just shook her head and laughed.

Once the four of them were seated, each feasting on a mound of ice cream smothered in various toppings, Sydney said, "Rachel, would you consider coming to the party with us?"

Her spoon had been poised midway between her dish and her mouth, but Rachel forgot all about luscious fudge sauce, so surprised was she by the question.

Sasha piped up, "Oh, you wouldn't be coming as a guest. You'd be a chaperone."

"I see."

Was that hesitation Rachel saw in Sophie's expression? But when next she looked, the child's face was filled with a smile, even if it was tight-lipped.

Sophie said, "Debbie's mother asked last week if some of the parents could come to help out, but... w-well...we didn't really want—"

Rachel smiled. "I understand. When you're twelve years old, adult supervision is the last thing you want."

She slipped the fudge-encrusted spoon between her lips and rolled the chocolate around in her mouth. After she swallowed, she asked, "But don't you think you ought to talk to your dad about this? His feelings might be hurt if you don't give him the opportunity to attend the party." She hastily added, "As a chaperone, of course."

The triplets looked at each other, and Rachel got the distinct impression that they were actually communicating by some sort of mental telepathy. It was silly, really, but then again, she'd read that identical siblings often had a special bond.

Finally, Sydney said, "Would you go?" She averted her gaze and added, "You know, if Dad says it's okay?"

Rachel looked down at her dish of ice cream, swirled her spoon in the whipped cream and nudged at the cherry as she dealt with the sudden emotion welling inside her.

Warmth filled her heart, and unexpected tears blurred her vision. The love she felt for these children was overwhelming at times. Here they were, getting ready to go to their first semiformal party, one of them even contemplating experiencing her very first kiss, and they were asking *her* to be a part of their special evening.

Memories bombarded Rachel. In the blink of an eye, she was standing beside her best friend's hospital bed, promising Olivia that she'd watch out for the girls. That she'd help to nurture them. That she'd do all she could to see to it that they grew into intelligent, well-rounded, happy individuals.

Olivia wasn't here to attend the triplets' first fancy party. Olivia couldn't snap any pictures of them all dressed up for the evening. Olivia couldn't give them advice about boys, or buy them pretty dresses, or act as a chaperone.

So Rachel would step forward and do all of these things.

"What's wrong?" Sophie asked, a frown biting deeply into her young brow.

"Why are you upset?" Sasha put her spoon down and stared at Rachel with worry in her gaze.

"I'm fine," Rachel assured them softly. "I was just thinking…"

She let the rest of her words trail off. The girls didn't need to be reminded of sad memories of their mother and what she and they were missing. No, this should be a joyful time for them.

"I was just thinking how happy I am that you asked me to go with you." She grinned at them. "I'd love to chaperone the party."

"Great!" Sydney said. "Now maybe Dad will let us stay out later than twelve-thirty."

Ah, Rachel thought, so the curfew had been what motivated them to invite her along. Leave it to practical, outspoken Sydney to burst Rachel's heartwarming fantasy of playing mommy.

But Rachel didn't feel hurt. She smiled, catching the eye of each one of them. The girls had no idea of the depth of her love for them, she was certain. She might not be their mother, she might not have given birth to them, but she sure did love them bunches and bunches. Like any mother loved her children.

Scooping up another spoonful of ice cream slathered with fudge sauce, Rachel said, "I can't promise you that your curfew will be any later. But I can promise you that I'll be at that party. With bells on!"

Sydney, Sophie and Sasha looked satisfied. Almost *too* satisfied.

Sloan looked in the mirror and straightened his tie. He was feeling pretty awkward about the New Year's Eve party he was about to chaperone for his daughters.

On the one hand, his heart felt all warm and mushy from his having been asked to attend. His emotions might have been categorized as something less than masculine by any male who wasn't a father. But he was sure dads all over the world would understand perfectly what he was going through. When the girls had approached him about chaperoning, their eyes had looked everywhere but at him, and their voices had been hesitant. They'd been as cute as little ladybugs. There had been no way he could have refused them.

But on the other hand, he'd be lying if he said he was really looking forward to this event.

His daughters would be laughing and gossiping, as girls their age were wont to do. However, they'd also be interacting with their friends. With *boys*. That idea just didn't sit well with him.

He wasn't a total idiot. He knew his girls had to grow up. But did they have to do it *now?*

Couldn't they wait? Like…a dozen or so years? Maybe then he'd be ready for this stage in their lives. As it was now, he wasn't prepared at all.

Then another question floated through his brain: was any father ever ready for his little girls to grow up? He seriously doubted it.

Scowling at his image in the mirror, he murmured, "Growing up, indeed."

His daughters were only twelve. They were too young for parties that would keep them out after their curfew. They were too young to be dancing with boys. Flirting with boys. Kissing boys—

He snapped off the thought as surely and as thoroughly as if it had been a lightbulb. He didn't mind plunging his brain into total darkness. Anything was better than continuing along this line of panic-inducing ponderings. If he didn't shut these thoughts down, he'd change his mind altogether and make Sydney, Sasha and Sophie ring in the New Year right here at home. And they'd never forgive him for that. Never.

So…how bad could the evening be? he wondered. He would be present at the party to watch all the goings-on. And when it came to his girls, he had the eye of an eagle.

The doorbell rang and Sloan grumbled under his breath. His daughters had probably offered one of their friends a lift to the party and had forgotten to tell him about it. He didn't mind. He only wished they would keep him apprised of the plans they made, then revamped, then revised yet again.

"Girls," he called down the hallway toward their rooms, "I'm going down to answer the door. You'd better hurry it up. It'll be time to go soon."

Sounds of frantic scrambling and panicked shrieks made him smile. One thing about his daughters, they could have five full hours to get themselves ready, and still they'd need more time.

He was still chuckling when he reached the front door and pulled it open. The sight he beheld made the grin on his face freeze as if his mouth had suddenly turned to solid concrete.

It was…it was…

Rachel smiled a silent greeting, stepped inside, closed the door behind her and then let her dress coat slide from her shoulders.

Thoughts refused to form coherently. Hell, they refused to form at all. It was as if his brain had completely shut down.

He took a deep breath. Forced himself to swallow. And blink, once, then again.

She looked too stunning for words.

Her flame-red hair—usually tamed by some sort of elastic band or hair clip when she was at the office—was wild about her shoulders, making for a very sultry look. This new do made her normally pale skin glow and look more delicate, more beautiful than he'd ever seen it.

At work, Rachel looked like any typical woman. However, tonight she'd done something to accentuate her brown eyes. He'd never realized before that her irises were flecked with a warm gold color that reminded him of heated honey. And her mouth. The bow was...utterly perfect. And he'd never seen her full bottom lip glisten so. The effect was...overwhelmingly kissable.

His mouth went dry at the thought, and he knew he should be ashamed of himself. But his mind was too busy with other things to take the time to do any silent berating.

Her black cocktail dress was shot through with silver threads, the fabric following the contours of her slender body. His gaze seemed to have a mind of its own as it roved down the length of her, over the swell of her breasts, the curve of her tiny waist that flowed right on down into flared hips.

An hourglass. She was a soft, luscious hourglass.

He choked as the startling thought lodged in his throat like some inhaled morsel of food.

Immediately, Rachel was clapping him on the back.

"You okay?" she asked, following him as he retreated into the living room.

If the truth were known, he was trying to flee. From what, he had no clue. But she stuck with him, following on those long, black-stocking-clad legs. She raised graceful, milky arms, and with her petite hands began slapping him soundly between the shoulder blades.

Aren't you cold? he wanted to ask. Didn't she know it was winter? Where were the sleeves of her dress? He'd never seen Rachel display so much... skin.

He worked with her in the office every single weekday. However, it was office policy that the employees wore colorful smocks over their attire. The nurses and office staff had a different color smock for every day of the week. He'd never realized just how shapeless those uniforms were. Before this moment, he'd never even realized that Rachel had a body.

Well, of course he'd known she'd had a body. He was a doctor, for goodness sake. But he never realized what a body she had!

Oh, hell.

Get a grip, he silently commanded himself. What on earth was the matter with him?

He needed to put a bit of space between them, that was all. He'd anticipated opening the door to one of his daughters' friends. He hadn't expected to see Rachel standing there at all. Her appearance had startled him.

Startled him? She'd shocked clear thinking right out of his brain. Like a solid whack with a sledgehammer right between the eyeballs.

"I'm fine," he told her, ducking to the left. "I'm okay."

As soon as he spoke, she stopped, and he continued on several paces just to give himself a little distance. Once he reached the couch, he paused to catch his breath, gather his wits. Only then did he turn to face her.

"You sure you're okay?"

The concern in her golden-bronze gaze affected him mightily. Usually, her interest was focused on his children. Rachel was their godmother. And she'd gone out of her way, especially since Olivia's death, to see that his girls were well-cared for. But recently she seemed more attached to his family than ever.

No, he silently answered her question. *I'm not at all sure that I'm okay.*

However, what he said was, "Sure. I'm fine. Just got a little choked up is all. I'm okay now. Really."

The entire time his mouth was uttering the words, he had to fight with his eyes to keep them focused on Rachel's face. His gaze kept wanting to slide down the length of her body, to get one more glimpse of those sinfully long and shapely legs of hers. Sometime during the last few frantic seconds, his subconscious must have noticed that the hem of her sexy little cocktail dress ended at midthigh. The urge to gape, stare, ogle, was pretty darned near overwhelming. He couldn't fathom what had gotten into him.

She sure did look like a million bucks. Certainly, to have realized that fact—obviously so, he was afraid—and not to comment on it would seem more than a little odd. So, tugging absently at the lapels of his jacket, he said, "Y-you, ah, you look great."

"So do you."

For the first time, he vaguely recognized that her gaze was clouded with what looked like confusion. A tiny crease marred the delicate skin between her eyes. However, he was still fighting off the strange effect her appearance had had on him, and that took so much effort that he didn't really have it in him to wonder too awfully much about what she might find bewildering.

"You obviously have plans tonight." As soon as he uttered the words, he was struck by the strangest feeling. An odd heaviness sat on his chest like a cement block.

"I was about to say the same thing to you."

Was that accusation he heard in her tone? he wondered. This whole situation had him feeling odd. Just a little off-kilter.

When he didn't answer, she said, "I'm going to the New Year's Eve party with the girls. They asked if I would help Debbie's mother by acting as a chaperone. And I agreed. I'm here to pick up the girls. Are they ready?" Then her head tilted and she asked, "They didn't tell you?"

Immediately upon hearing that Rachel would be attending the same party as he, the bizarre heaviness seemed to evaporate. What took its place was a curious lightness that wafted around him like sweet, candy-scented air. But he no more understood this sugary feeling than he did the other emotions that had reached up out of nowhere to grab at him.

What was wrong with his central nervous system? Was he coming down with a cold?

"No," he told her, feeling preoccupied with the emotions churning inside him. "The girls never said a word." He felt his brow furrow with uncertainty. Why hadn't the girls let him know they had asked Rachel to go to the party?

Kids. Would they ever become responsible for their actions?

Now, Rachel looked as if she felt awkward.

"Y-you," she stammered hesitantly, "look as if you have plans for the evening. Are you going out?"

Then he chuckled, nodding ironically. "I'm going to the party, too."

The glow he had noticed seemed to fade and Rachel's face suddenly took on an ashen shade.

"You are?"

"Uh-huh," he told her softly. "I am. They asked me today. I guess the three of them somehow got their signals crossed."

"But they were all together when..." Rachel's thought seemed to peter out, and she shook her head. "It doesn't matter," she said.

A sudden thought struck him. "Look, since I'm going...there's really no need for you to be troubled—"

"But, *Dad!*"

"We *want* Rachel to go—"

"She's gotta go, Dad. Debbie's mom is expecting her help."

Sloan turned to see his daughters standing at the foot of the stairs.

The first things he noticed were their expressions. Surreptitious. Sly. Even *sneaky* wouldn't have been too harsh a word to describe the looks in their eyes. What were they up to?

Before he could give the question the attention it deserved, he noticed their attire. His little girls were beautiful in their party dresses and fancy shoes. Looking all grown-up. Their long, dark hair glistening. His mouth opened, his breath leaving him in a rush.

His daughters were lovely. Lovely enough to make

everything else slide into the background of his brain as his heart contracted with love.

Music blared at an earsplitting level. Sloan positioned himself at the very back of the large banquet room in order to save his hearing. He couldn't believe how elaborate the party decorations were. Mrs. Fox, Debbie's mother, had gone to great lengths to make her daughter's New Year's Eve bash a success.

Colorful helium balloons bobbed from ribbons anchored to every conceivable surface. Streamers were draped from the corners of the room, some of them dangling straight down from the ceiling, making a sort of obstacle course that the kids seemed to love. The tables were covered with cloths that had been sprinkled with shimmering confetti. One long table was weighed down with food and beverages. The dance floor was lit from above with rainbow lighting, and the tunes were being played by a professional disc jockey. A professional DJ for twelve-year-olds?

Yes, quite a bit of money had been paid out for this affair.

Sloan was surprised by the number of children milling around. One group of kids ambled by him, and not one of them even acknowledged him with a look, let alone a verbal greeting. Ah, well, he thought, they were off in their own world. A world that didn't include chaperones. He chuckled to himself.

He was feeling so…odd. And he couldn't quite put his finger on why.

Lighthearted. Gleeful, even. The music was deafening, yes, and the pop tunes were definitely not his favorite style. But he'd found himself tapping his toes to the beat a time or two.

However, along with this peculiar breeziness, he also felt a sense of foreboding. He couldn't help thinking that something was about to happen. Often he was struck by a feeling of premonition. And when he got that feeling, it usually wasn't long before he received a call from his answering service with a message from a patient who needed him. He hated the idea of being called away from the triplets' big night out. But if that were to happen, Rachel was here to save the day—or rather, the evening—for the girls.

Yes, something strange was in the air. That was certain. And he was struck by yet another odd sensation—that whatever it was had something to do with Rachel.

The thought of her had him scanning the room. It took no time at all to find her in the crowd. In fact, it was almost as if his subconscious had been keeping tabs on Rachel's location—and the location of his daughters—ever since the five of them had arrived.

As usual, Rachel had pitched in right away, helping Mrs. Fox with various jobs. She'd laughed with the kids, who didn't seem to ignore her the way they ignored him. She'd even dragged some of the girls and boys out onto the dance floor when no one had seemed willing to start the party rolling. Her shoulders had shimmied as she'd danced, her fanny swaying to the rhythm of the music. That sight had had him suppressing a smile, and reaching to loosen the collar of his shirt.

Even now, as he thought of it, his toe began to tap

lightly, a grin tugging at one corner of his mouth. He could almost feel his blood pressure rising, although Rachel was no longer dancing, but filling up cups with punch for some thirsty adolescents.

Lord, she sure looked good—

"Dr. Radcliff—"

Sloan started, not realizing just how mesmerized he'd become by his surveillance of Rachel—by his surveillance of *everyone,* he silently and swiftly corrected the thought. It was his job to chaperone, wasn't it?

"Mrs. Fox," he said, greeting her with a nod.

"Please call me Virginia. Our daughters have been friends for too long for us to be so formal."

He smiled. "All right, Virginia. And you can call me Sloan."

"I'd love to."

The unexpected sultry quality of her voice made him pause. Then he said, "Great party you've put on here. The kids are really enjoying themselves."

"You think so?"

Anxiety tinged her blue eyes, clouding them a little. Again, he nodded his assurance.

"I came over—"

Her hand slid over his forearm as she spoke, and Sloan was engulfed by the urge to step away from the woman. Even though he didn't back up an inch, she still moved closer to him, almost as if she sensed his impulse to retreat.

"—to thank you for coming to help," she purred.

Her smile was so warm it could have melted asphalt. He was actually taken aback. He was struck by the thought that Virginia Fox was some kind of

Amazon huntress—and he was most definitely the prey. He'd never actually been made to feel like wild game before, caught in the crosshairs. This was a first.

She cast a quick glance over her shoulder and then turned to face him again, whispering, "After the party, do you think you might like to go out—" another covert scan of the room "—and have a drink?"

He did lean away from her now as he tried to control his astonishment.

"Won't it be awfully late?" The question rolled from his tongue before he could think of anything else to say. "Besides, my girls will need me to…I'll need to see that they…"

He was flabbergasted by the woman's suggestion. They both had children that needed tending. How could she think he could leave them home alone in the middle of the night?

She waved away his pitiful excuses. "You can get that secretary of yours—what's her name? Raquel?—to take care of them for you." Virginia cast another glance around the party. "She seems nice enough. Competent, even." The woman's voice dropped an octave as she added, "If you like the flamboyant type, that is."

Flamboyant? Rachel?

Sloan wanted to burst out laughing.

Granted, Rachel's hair was a little wild tonight. But everyone was allowed to let their hair down every now and then, weren't they? And, yes, that dress… The mere thought of it had him mentally shaking his head in wonder. If the black-and-silver fabric had any sense at all it would be deliriously happy to be snuggling against Rachel's luscious curves.

He was definitely losing his grip. These sexual thoughts about his office manager were growing more curious and more unrestrained as the evening wore on.

Virginia's hand slid up his arm, her fingers squeezing his biceps suggestively.

"Come on," she breathed. "Having a drink together will be fun."

He'd met Debbie's mother at school functions a few times, but she'd never approached him in such an intimate manner before. He hated to hurt the woman's feelings, but he just wasn't interested—

"Hey, Dad."

Sloan had never been happier to see anyone in all his born days as he was to see Sophie right now. Rachel was with his daughter, and Sloan seized the opportunity to extricate himself from Virginia's possessive clutches.

"Hi, honey," Sloan greeted his daughter. "You having a good time?"

"Yeah." She cut her eyes up at Mrs. Fox who took a backward step, at least having enough sense to look chagrined. "Thanks for the party, Mrs. F."

"Why, you're welcome…which one are you?" She then laughed nervously as she looked at Sloan. "I can never tell your girls apart."

"I'm Sophie," his daughter provided.

Her mind obviously on other things, Virginia ignored the child completely, plastered on a smile and commented without much enthusiasm, "Why, look, Raquel brought us some punch. How nice."

"It's Rachel," Sophie automatically corrected. "And the punch is for Dad."

Rachel smiled apologetically at the woman. Handing the cup to Sloan, she said, "Sophie thought you might be thirsty."

After a little shuffling that his daughter had seemed to initiate, Sloan found himself standing close to Rachel. Very close.

Rachel looked down at Sophie. "There's plenty of room. No need to crowd your father."

"Thanks," he said. He looked down into the red fruity drink, but the awkwardness of the moment kept him from enjoying a sip.

Then Sophie blurted, "Dad, are you planning to dance tonight?"

He grinned down at her. "Is that an invitation?"

"Ick! No way!" she screeched. Then she let out a snort of laughter. "The kids really would think I'm a geek if I danced with my father. Bobby's waiting for me." She smiled up at him. "I thought you might like to ask Rachel."

What an idea! he thought. He could have hugged Sophie for giving him a great excuse for escaping Virginia—and the perfect justification for holding Rachel in his arms. At that very moment, he realized that was what he'd been wanting to do ever since she'd shown up on his doorstep looking gorgeous.

"Thanks for the suggestion, honey," he told his daughter. Then he teased, "But…are the chaperones allowed to dance? I wouldn't want to embarrass you."

"Just so long as you don't start acting goofy," was Sophie's response.

He chuckled. "I promise to restrain myself." Then he looked at Rachel, "Would you like to dance?"

Her honey-brown eyes filled with pleasant surprise, and she nodded.

He grinned at her, then turned to Virginia. "Here. Enjoy this while I'm gone."

Then, leaving the blonde holding his punch cup with her red-painted mouth partly open in disbelief, he led Rachel toward the dance floor.

Chapter Three

Heaven couldn't be more wonderful than this. Cradled in Sloan's strong, protective arms, Rachel felt as if she were in paradise. The slow music wrapped around them, enfolded them in the most sensuous rhythm imaginable.

She'd known Sloan for years, so it wasn't as if they'd never had the opportunity to be close. She was the godmother of his daughters. His deceased wife's best friend. She'd helped him nurse Olivia until the bitter end. And she worked with him daily as she managed his medical office. She supposed he considered her his friend—although she'd always wanted to be so much more than that. However, being friends meant they celebrated nearly every holiday together. There were birthday hugs and Christmas kisses, quick displays of friendly affection that always took place in the blink of an eye. The number of times that the two of them had slow-danced together could be counted on one of Rachel's hands.

At Sloan's wedding—oh-so-many years ago—Rachel had found herself in his arms...and it had been the most awkward moment she'd ever lived through. The circumstances had been tense. For everyone concerned. Rachel could close her eyes right now and easily remember the strain visible on Sloan's handsome face on the day he had wed Olivia. Rachel's heart had ached for him, and she'd been furious with Olivia and her conniving ways. No one deserved the treatment she had inflicted on—

Sloan's hand slid down the length of Rachel's back, nestling lightly on the curve of her spine, causing her heart to flutter, and knocking her out of the awful reverie of the past. Rachel hated the silly, schoolgirl reaction that overwhelmed her each and every time she was near Sloan. You'd think her physical response to him would have diminished with time, especially since he didn't seem to be affected by her—attracted to her—in the least. However, the emotions that stirred in her when she was near him hadn't abated one bit over the years. Not one tiny bit.

Defeating the silly feelings had been impossible. She'd tried hard to do just that. By ignoring them. Mentally stomping on them. Ranting and raving against them when she was all alone in her apartment, among other things. Nothing had worked. Nothing. So she'd simply decided to suffer them in silence.

Again, his fingers played over the small of her

back. She was so conscious of his touch. It was rare that she felt his hands on her.

The warmth of his skin through the fabric of her dress made her pulse heat. Her stomach seemed to twist and turn in somersaults, but she did her best to keep her gaze averted, focusing on moving smoothly across the floor and not stepping on his toes. That would be embarrassing.

Something stirred her consciousness. He was staring at her, willing her to lift her gaze to his. She could sense it. Strongly. Excitement skittered across her nerve endings like so many pinpricks. She tried to tamp it down, but it was a fruitless effort.

Slowly she tipped up her chin…and immediately found herself lost in his dark gaze.

Why, oh, why did he have to be so handsome? Why were his eyes such a tempting shade of brown, like irresistible bittersweet chocolate? Why did he have to smell so luscious, like some hot and mysterious tropical night when just about anything could happen? She gave her head an almost imperceptible shake as she attempted to banish the fanciful thoughts from her mind.

But the cut of his slate-gray suit accentuated his broad, powerful shoulders. The teal tie with its impressionistic design looked elegant against the crisp white dress shirt. How could a woman not feel awed by such a good-looking man?

Then she noticed it. That strange twinkle in his eyes.

Words tumbled from her mouth as quickly as her brain conjured them. "You look like you're up to something. What are you thinking?"

His shoulders rose a fraction as he flawlessly guided her around the dance floor. "I was just wondering, is all."

"Wondering?" she asked, her curiosity really piqued now. "Wondering what?"

For a moment, he looked as if he intended to avoid answering her question. But then he seemed to surrender to the gaiety of the evening, his gaze glittering with lighthearted enjoyment, and he grinned.

The sexiness of it just about made her panty hose roll down to her knees.

"I was wondering," he told her, "why a beautiful woman like you has never settled down. Why haven't you found yourself a husband, Rachel?"

So stunned was she by his query, her eyes snapped wide open, and she planted the sole of her shoe directly on top of his foot. He managed to chuckle through a grimace.

"Oh, my," she murmured, missing the humor he evidently saw in her clumsiness. "Sorry."

"No problem."

She didn't know what made her flush more, the fact that she'd squashed his foot beneath hers, or the thought of revealing the truthful answer to the question he'd posed.

For years after he and Olivia had married, Rachel had done everything she could to meet a man who might capture her affection—and take her attention off her best friend's husband. She'd dated more men than she could count. But none of them seemed to hold a candle to Sloan. She'd grown weary of the hunt. Then Olivia had gotten sick and needed her. And after their mother's death, the triplets had needed Rachel's help through the overwhelming grief they had suffered. Without conscious thought, Rachel had allowed the idea of dating to fall by the wayside as she grew content with her work in the doctors' office and spending time with Sydney, Sasha and Sophie.

Rachel didn't feel she had a bad life. In fact, her days were rather full, with her job and with the girls. However, in all honesty, her nights could use a little filling. But she couldn't see herself admitting *that* piece of information to Sloan. No way!

"So?" The expression in his eyes was as unrelenting as the tone of his voice.

Oh, Lord, help me, she silently prayed. He really did expect a response from her.

Her gaze darted off over his shoulder as she said, "I guess the right man just hasn't come along." For good measure, she added, "Yet."

As lies went, it wasn't all that huge. The right man *had* come along, all right, but if he didn't feel the same kind of attraction—the same kind of magnetism that she was experiencing—then there wasn't a whole lot she could do about the situation.

Pondering her intense feelings for Sloan caused a dark guilt to envelop her. A guilt that was so familiar, it felt like a well-worn coat when it wrapped itself around her. She had no business feeling anything for Sloan. No business at all.

At that instant, the slow tune faded and he released her. But, immediately, another song came blaring from the speakers. At the sound of Chubby Checker and "The Twist," Sloan's mouth quirked with a grin that was so fun-loving, so charming, it stole her breath away.

"What do you say?" he asked, his dark brows waggling in invitation.

His voice was filled with such joviality that Rachel couldn't help but accept his offer with a nod and a laugh. The guilt that had descended just a moment before evaporated the instant she began swiveling her hips to the rhythm of the music. There was a flurry of movement as children swarmed onto the dance floor all around them.

It didn't seem possible for such a tall, broad-framed man to move with such elegance and grace. At one point, he bent his knees, hunkered down, twisting lower and lower. His eyes lit with a playful challenge. Rachel threw her head back and laughed. Then she, too, crouched low, her hips swiveling in one direction, her hands and knees in the other. Grinning like precocious kids, they danced close, their shoulders nearly touching as they raised themselves back to a standing position.

Unexpectedly, Sloan grabbed her hand, twirled her in a circle, and they continued to twist with their fingers laced together.

"Anyone ever tell you that you're a wonderful dancer?" she asked.

"I'm a little rusty," he commented over the music. "But I'm having a great time."

Rachel nodded. "Me, too."

"I sure hope the girls don't think I'm acting goofy," he said, grinning.

She laughed. "They're so busy dancing, I don't think they've even noticed that we're out here."

Just then, the fast tune faded, to be replaced by yet another slow song.

"It's good that they haven't noticed," he said, pulling her against him, "because I'd forgotten how fun acting goofy can be."

The room suddenly felt close, the air warm. Sure, she was flushed and out of breath from all the swinging and twirling and laughing they'd just done, but something told her the change she'd noticed had nothing to do with their playful antics.

Was it her imagination, or was he holding her just a little tighter than he had during their first slow dance of the evening?

He was so close. Too close for her to feel comfortable, pressed against his chest. However, this discomfort was delicious.

She hadn't a clue what had gotten into him, but, admittedly, this was even better than the paradise she'd entered when he'd first held her tonight. His arms were so snug around her, his face so close to hers. *This* was pure, unadulterated ecstasy.

Delight swelled from somewhere inside her, swirling and churning, rising like a tide. It would be utterly foolish of her to drown in all this wonderment, no matter how much she wanted to. She grinned up at him, desperately striving to hold on to the lighthearted merriment that the fast music had conjured between them. But the feeling of fun and frivolity was nowhere to be found in his eyes. Their expression was…intense. He'd never looked at her like this before. Her mind went blank with anxiety and she was, all at once, certain she'd forgotten how to draw a breath. If he kept gazing at her so fixedly, she was sure she'd suffocate and fall to the floor in a dead faint.

"You shouldn't be spending New Year's Eve at a party with a bunch of children," he whispered. "You should be off somewhere romantic. Being wined and dined. Wooed by a man who's wearing his heart on his sleeve. You deserve more than this, Rachel. Much more."

His words touched her heart. He was so sweet. Like those expensive, imported chocolate truffles that no woman could get enough of.

A smile curled the corners of her mouth. Without thinking, she said, "But this is exactly where I want to be."

The honesty of her statement and the sultriness in her voice had her blinking in surprise. Had she really revealed herself so blatantly? What would he think?

But her sensuous tone didn't seem to have the same effect on him. Surprise was evidently the last thing he was feeling at the moment. In fact, he suddenly looked mesmerized by her mouth. The strains of the slow tune seemed to recede as he stared at her lips, ran the backs of his fingers along her cheek, then twisted his hand, his fingers capturing her jaw in a gentle grip.

Oh. *Oh*. Was he really going to—

His mouth slanted down over hers. His kiss was hot, moist, as his tongue skipped lightly, languidly across her lips. Instinct alone made her lean into him, press her body to his, but before she had time to react further, he lifted his face away from hers, breaking off the kiss.

Now he was clearly surprised. The astonishment

written on his striking features was so complete—so much like what she was feeling—that Rachel nearly gasped. The two of them not only stopped dancing, but they stepped apart as they continued to gawk at each other in disbelief.

Embarrassment flooded her face with rosy heat, and her heart pumped so fiercely that she no longer heard the music at all, only the thump, thump, thump of her pulse resounding in her ears like some runaway, totally maniacal drumbeat.

Self-consciousness made them both peer around to see who might be watching.

"The girls," Sloan murmured worriedly, shooting a quick glance in one direction, then the other.

But no one, neither the adolescents attending the party nor the adults chaperoning the affair, seemed to be paying them much mind. Even the hostess, Virginia, was fully absorbed in the task of refreshing the punch bowl.

"I think we're okay."

He whispered the words with clear relief, catching her eye at the same time. As he sucked in a breath, his face registered sudden alarm.

"It's not that I'm embarrassed…"

Shaking her head, she told him, "It's okay. I understand."

Rachel found herself being led from the dance floor toward the far end of the room.

"Like I said…it's not that I'm embarrassed."

Once they reached their destination, a quiet, relatively uninhabited corner, he turned to face her. And it was obvious that he was feeling utterly miserable.

"Who am I kidding?" he said. "I'm terribly embarrassed. Rachel, I'm sorry. How could I have done such a thing?''

That final question seemed to be asked of himself rather than her.

She wished he hadn't apologized. That kiss had been wonderful. Yes, it had been surprising. But wonderful, nonetheless.

"Can you forgive me?" he continued. "I just don't know what got into me. I'm so sorry. I just can't imagine—"

"Sloan…please."

Every time he apologized, she felt more awkward about what had just transpired between them.

"It's been such a long time since I've—" he shook his head "—had so much fun with anyone." Reaching up, he raked agitated fingers through his hair. "It's been such a long time since I've—" again he paused, shrugging "—danced with a woman. Can you forgive me, Rachel? I'm really, *really* sorry."

The level of her torment rose yet another notch. Why couldn't he see what his profuse apologies were doing to her?

Because she refused to allow him to see, she told herself. She wasn't going to lose all dignity. Not over a little, meaningless kiss, anyway. Closing her eyes, she struggled not to think about just how meaningful that kiss was to her.

"Really," he repeated.

The tension between them thickened to the consistency of wet cement until Rachel felt both of them were trudging through it waist-deep.

Just then the DJ announced, "Are we ready to ring

in the new year? It'll be here in five seconds. Four, three, two, one. Happy New Year!''

The kids in the room screamed and laughed, clapped and shouted in celebration.

But it was as if a black cloud had descended on Rachel and Sloan. A cloud that blocked every bit of revelry from them as they stood together, apart from the festivities, looking completely regretful.

This New Year's party would be remembered by Rachel as being both the best and the worst she'd ever experienced. The best, because of the blissful slow dances, not to mention the delectable, spontaneous kiss she and Sloan had shared. And the worst, because she knew without a doubt that Sloan wished that kiss had never happened.

The first business day of the new year dawned crisp and clear. Rachel unlocked the front door of the building, snapping on lights as she made her way through the offices. She liked arriving a good twenty to thirty minutes before the doctors and nurses. The extra time gave her a chance to start a pot of coffee brewing in the employee kitchen, go through the mail and make certain that all the supply requests were filled.

She loved running Sloan's office. Well, it was also Travis and Greg's practice, too. Her job was pretty much her life. Her job, and her goddaughters.

They had spent part of New Year's Day together at Travis Westcott's house. The twin Native American boys Travis had adopted, Josh and Jared, had had their naming ceremony, presided over by an actual medicine woman from the Kolheek tribe.

The ritual had fascinated Rachel. The boys, and Travis, too, had received beautiful Indian names. Diana Chapman, the medicine woman, had looked serene and beautiful in her beaded doeskin dress, her long black hair shining in the firelight. And the small fire wasn't the only thing heating up the evening. During the celebratory meal after the ceremony, Rachel had been certain that sparks of attraction were flying between Travis and Diana.

And Jane and Greg, the newlyweds of the group, had been so focused on each other that they hadn't noticed the tension between Rachel and Sloan. Well, that was all for the best, Rachel thought. She wouldn't want her other two bosses suspecting that something inappropriate was going on between her and Sloan.

However, at the get-together, the triplets had noticed something was amiss. Sophie had asked Rachel if she and Sloan had had an argument. Rachel had successfully sidetracked the child by asking if Bobby Snyders had actually garnered the nerve to kiss her the night before at the party. And Sophie had forgotten all about her suspicions regarding trouble between Rachel and her father, launching into a gushing soliloquy of how wonderful her experience had been. In the end, she'd become so dramatic, Rachel teasingly accused her of taking acting lessons from Sasha and asked if, since receiving Bobby's kiss, she planned never to wash her face again. Of course, Sophie had been indignant at first, but then she'd ended up laughing right along with Rachel.

The laughter she'd shared with the child had been about the only lighthearted part of the evening. Sloan would have been a terrible poker player, because he certainly wasn't any good at hiding his feelings from the world. It was clear to her—and to everyone else, she was sure—that he was distressed. She knew the kiss they had shared during the party was what had upset him, but she sure didn't want everyone else to know about it. At Travis's house, they had ended up avoiding each other all evening long, and in a group that small, doing so hadn't been easy.

Travis entered the front door of the office suite just as Rachel was booting up her computer.

"Good morning," she greeted him. "You're in awfully early."

He was grinning from ear to ear. "I'm ready to get to work."

His demeanor made her smile, too. "That's good. A doctor waiting for patients. Now, *that's* a switch."

Travis chuckled. The chest-high counter separated them. He leaned over it, placing his hand flat on the top, and said, "Can I tell you a secret?"

"I love secrets."

The joy he felt couldn't be contained. "Diana and I have...reached an understanding."

Not exactly sure what Travis was revealing, Rachel waited, hoping he'd elaborate. He didn't disappoint her.

"She won't be going back to the reservation." His smile widened further as he professed, "I've asked her to marry me...and she said yes."

"Oh, Travis!" She rounded the counter and hugged him. "That's wonderful."

Just then, Greg arrived.

"Boy," Rachel said, "looks like everyone's coming in early. Have you heard the good news? Travis and Diana are planning a wedding. Pretty soon you won't be the only newlywed around here."

"Congratulations!" Greg pumped Travis's hand and then wrapped his arms around him in a back-slapping bear hug. "When's the happy event?"

"Sometime in the spring, I guess," Travis said. He turned to Rachel. "Diana would like you to take her shopping. She's new to the area, you know. And it would be nice if you could show her around town."

"I'd love to," Rachel told him. "Greg, maybe Jane would like to go. I'll give her a call."

"Speaking of Jane," Greg said, "I'm expecting her lab results back...."

"Right here." Rachel reached down, picked up a large gray envelope and handed it to him.

"Great! Listen—"

A gust of cold wind preceded Sloan into the front office. "Greg. Travis." He followed up the greeting with a curt nod. "Any messages for me, Rachel?"

Why...he couldn't even look her in the eye. She hurried around the counter to her desk, embarrassment tingeing her cheeks with crimson. Surely, Greg and Travis would notice his strange behavior.

Scrambling to gather the messages she'd retrieved from their answering service, Rachel picked out the yellow slips belonging to him and passed them over the counter.

He didn't even thank her. He just continued on down the hall. The three of them heard his door close.

"What's eating him?" Travis asked.

"How should *I* know?" Her face flamed again at the defensiveness in her tone.

Greg and Travis turned their gazes on her at the same time.

She groaned inwardly. If Sloan's demeanor didn't start the gossip mill, her own would. Especially since Travis had been looking at Greg when he asked the question.

She needed to deal with this. Now. Normally, Rachel didn't have a confrontational bone in her body. But if she didn't speak to Sloan about the way he was treating her, everyone in the office would be wondering…and talking.

"Will you two excuse me?" she said, doing her best to remain calm. "I need to take care of something."

The men nodded in acknowledgment; however, as she walked away from them, it was quite easy for her to imagine them sharing a curious look.

Shaking her head, she realized that now she was getting paranoid, which was all the more reason for her to speak with Sloan. Up until this moment, she'd enjoyed a comfortable work environment. She didn't want that to change.

Rachel knocked, but didn't wait for Sloan to respond before she charged into his office. He looked up from across the room, the sight of her making his dark eyes grow hooded.

"Would you please cut it out?" she hissed. Without allowing him time to respond, she continued, "I realize that you regret kissing me. But it was *just a kiss,* for goodness' sake. It's not like we rolled around naked on that dance floor on New Year's Eve.

Stop feeling so darned guilty! It was a simple kiss. It meant nothing. I will not have everyone whispering about the way you're treating me. Like I've got some contagious disease or something.'' In a huff, she added, "Please remember that we have to work together. And we're not the only two people in this office!''

With that, she turned on her heel and left him with his mouth agape.

Chapter Four

Later that same week, Sloan sat at his desk pondering the fact that everything and everyone in his life was changing.

Over the past two months, not one but both his partners had found love. Joy emanated from Greg like a fantastic laser-light show since he'd taken Jane as his wife. And ever since Travis had asked Diana to become his bride, he, too, seemed to be walking on clouds.

Having attended medical school with these men as well as having worked in this practice with them, Sloan felt he knew his friends pretty well. However, the idea that they had both tumbled head over feet in love in such a short period of time still threw him for a loop. Oh, he was pleased that they were happy. What kind of friend would he be to feel anything else? However, they had seemed so content as bachelors, and Sloan had thought that all three of them had been muddling through life fairly well on their own—without the complications of romantic entanglements.

Well, he silently surmised, nothing and no one stayed the same forever.

Boy, that went for his daughters, too. The changes his girls were going through lately were phenomenal. He could clearly see the triplets' teen years were going to cause him some misery and mental anguish. The girls were becoming more and more rebellious with each day that passed. Querulous. Self-centered. Demanding. Those adjectives could probably be used to describe any and all preteens in this day and age. However, dealing with his tireless trio made him feel as if he were constantly caught in the crosshairs of a triple-barrel shotgun. Okay, okay, so there wasn't such a thing as a triple-barrel shotgun. Still, he felt the metaphor fit Sasha, Sophie and Sydney. Perfectly.

Yes, everything was changing. Even his relationship with Rachel was going through some sort of strange but distinct transformation. He couldn't quite put his finger on the why, but there was such an amazing shift in how he saw the woman—in how he *thought* of her—that it was absolutely impossible to deny.

Rachel had been Olivia's best friend since before he'd even entered the picture. Even all those years ago, he had never been quite able to figure out how the two of them had become so close. They were as different as night and day. Rachel had grown up in a family that, from what he could tell, had struggled to make ends meet, while Olivia's father had amassed quite a fortune in various business ventures.

Rachel had been studious, but hadn't been able to afford anything more than the local community college. Olivia's family could have afforded Vanderbilt, Vassar or any institution in between; however, Olivia hadn't cared one whit about traveling the scholarly path. After meeting Sloan, all she'd focused on was pressuring him into marriage so she could have a home, a white picket fence and children.

Sloan closed his eyes, his brow furrowing. As with any other time, thinking of his deceased wife conjured up a multitude of dark and complicated emotions: resentment, guilt, anger, regret. He did his best to push the feelings to the back of his mind. The thing he wanted to focus on at the moment was his relationship with Rachel and how it had changed of late.

He'd have liked to say that he'd never thought of Rachel in any vein other than as Olivia's best friend and his daughters' godmother, but that would be a lie. Years ago, before he and Olivia had married, Sloan had admired Rachel when he'd met her. She'd had such a determination to succeed. An ambition to finish school, no matter what or how. And he'd even felt a spark of attraction. However, he'd already begun dating Olivia at the time, and he couldn't very well have acted on his feelings without hurting both Olivia and Rachel. Coming between best friends wasn't something a gentleman would consider.

Again, he found himself tamping down guilt that was dark and dank. He couldn't fathom why he felt guilty. It wasn't as if he'd acted on his feelings for Rachel. Heck, he hadn't even had the chance to contemplate whatever attraction he might have felt for her because, in the blink of an eye, fate—and his own poor judgment—had swept them all into the swift current of life-altering change. He'd quickly found himself married to Olivia and the father of triplet girls.

He'd done the right thing back then. Taking responsibility for his actions had been the only choice in his mind. And he'd been too busy trying to earn a living and provide for his family to be concerned with much else. Then, when he'd just about come to the depressing conclusion that he was heading toward a dim future filled with manual-labor jobs and mediocre pay, Olivia had urged him to go back to school…and the rest was history.

When Olivia had gotten sick, Sloan had already finished his medical training and was just setting up the practice he shared with Greg and Travis. Thankfully, Rachel had been there to help, with his desperately ill wife, the triplet toddlers *and* the newly formed medical practice. When he was at the office, Rachel had been with his family and vice versa. He'd never have gotten through those awful months without her. And when Olivia had died…well, Sloan was sure his girls would never have made it through their grief without Rachel.

The woman had been a godsend.

And ever since his girls had contracted this horrible disease called preteen adolescence, Rachel had once again been close at hand to lend support and offer help. Sloan was mightily grateful.

Since his wife's death, he'd been too focused on playing the hand destiny had dealt him to do anything more than fly through life by the seat of his pants. He'd concentrated on raising his daughters and building his practice. He hadn't really had time to deal with his own grief, not to mention the other confusing emotions that were associated with Olivia. And due to the very dark and complicated feelings, he hadn't dared to allow himself to see Rachel as anything other than what she was: a caring friend to him and his daughters. A friend who also happened to be an employee.

However, having seen Rachel in that tight black dress on New Year's Eve, having held her in his arms on the dance floor, having kissed her luscious lips…

Sloan swallowed painfully and scrubbed his hand over his face as he sat listening to the quiet of his office. That evening they'd spent together had changed everything.

Everything.

Whenever they were in the same room together, the atmosphere took on the earmarks of a full-fledged Independence Day celebration, complete with noisy and colorful fireworks. The very air became so charged it seemed nearly impossible to draw a breath. Never in his life had he experienced such a phenomenon.

He had to face the facts. The flicker of attraction he'd once felt for Rachel had returned. But it was no longer simply a flicker. It had grown to the size of a red-hot, five-alarm fire—a fire that seemed impossible to extinguish.

Rachel hesitated before knocking on the door of Sloan's office. Approaching Sloan was something she always seemed to do with foot-dragging reluctance—not because she was unwilling to interact with him or spend time with him, but because she was afraid she was *too* willing to do those things, and that her eagerness would be noted by everyone at the office, including Sloan himself.

A pink-smocked nurse passed her in the hallway, acknowledging her with a quick nod. Rachel returned the woman's smile, feeling extremely self-conscious at having been caught loitering just outside Sloan's office.

It was that darned kiss that was to blame for this awful ill-at-ease feeling she'd been suffering of late. Sure, she'd always been careful that her co-workers didn't discover her attraction to Sloan, but she'd never really felt paranoid before. And that's exactly what she felt each and every time someone shot her a look or a smile these days.

Quickly, she rapped on the door and then pushed her way inside. Awareness skipped across her every nerve ending when she saw him across the room.

He was just replacing the telephone receiver into its cradle. The scowl marring his forehead disturbed her.

"Is everything okay?" she found herself asking automatically.

He shook his head with a sigh. "No. I'm afraid it's not." He indicated the phone with a tilt of his head. "That was the principal at the girls' school. Seems they'll be spending time in detention this afternoon after classes. They were caught loafing in the rest room before fifth period. This was the third time this week it's happened. And Mrs. Harris didn't come right out and accuse the girls of smoking cigarettes, but she did say the room was as smoggy as the Blue Route during rush hour. Apparently, my girls weren't the only students involved. The whole lot will be spending an hour after school being lectured on the hazards of smoking. And being late for class. I'll have to make a special trip over there to pick them up." Again, he sighed. Softly, almost to himself, he asked, "What is going on here? What's happening to my daughters?"

"Oh, Sloan." Rachel shook her head, commiserating with him. She eased herself into the chair opposite his desk. "I can't imagine the girls smoking. It's a disgusting habit. But...if they did," she added a quick shrug, "it is...well, a normal thing for a kid to try, don't you think?"

"Their father's a doctor, Rachel," Sloan lamented. "They know the health risks involved with tobacco use. They know I've lost patients to lung cancer. They're smart kids. I just don't get it."

"I agree on both counts. They are smart." Then she felt the need to remind him, "But they *are* kids."

His dark eyes were intense as he evidently waited for her to elaborate her thoughts.

"Kids can't see themselves coming down with any kind of disease," she explained. "Kids live for today. Illness is only for old fogies like you and me." She grinned in an attempt to lighten the mood, but her smile faded almost instantly when she saw that her humor had fallen flat.

"Come on, now," she said softly. "This isn't all that bad. You'll ground them this coming weekend. Invent some extra hard chores for them to do as part of their punishment. Make them scrub the toilets with a toothbrush. Worse yet, make them shovel out their rooms. Keeping them away from the mall will be enough to teach them a lesson. It's going to be okay.'' Again, she offered him a soft smile. ''Look at it this way…you should be glad that they were caught and that they're spending time in detention, listening to the principal's punishing lectures. Now that you know what's going on, you can deal with it.''

His mouth set into a long, hard line. ''The trouble is, there's been a lot to deal with lately. And I don't think I've been reacting to their escapades the way a good father should. The way an understanding father would.''

Surprise had her brows shooting toward the ceiling. ''You don't really believe that, do you? You're a great dad.'' It seemed important to somehow back up the compliment. ''I mean, I know I don't have kids of my own…so I don't know a whole lot about parenting. But…if I did have kids—'' her words came in a rush ''—I'd love for you to be their father.''

Her eyes widened, her mouth formed a surprised *O* before she had a chance to stop herself. Had those words really tumbled from her mouth?

''What I mean is,'' she rushed to amend, ''I'd let you father my children any day—''

No, no, no! a silent voice roared at her. That comment had been even worse. Sweat prickled across her brow, her heart hammered, her face flushed. That wasn't at all what she'd meant.

''What I *intended* to say,'' she tried yet again,

"was that..." Words whirled in her brain so fast, she couldn't seem to pin down the right ones.

She made one last attempt. "You're a *good* father, Sloan. You love your girls. You try as hard as you can. No one could say you don't."

Her blundering attempt to praise him had obviously startled him as much as it had her.

"Thanks, but—" his gaze was averted as he shook his head "—not everyone would approve of my parental skills." His tone was tinged with regret as he added, "Olivia would be very disappointed."

Rachel's heart about broke in two when she heard that. Suddenly, her chin was tipping up in a most unusual manner and she found herself saying, "Well, you know something, Sloan...Olivia isn't here." Then she quickly pointed out, "You are."

For some reason, she got a sudden and uncomfortable sense that she was somehow condemning her friend, and that allowed guilt to tweak at her. However, her purpose had been to encourage Sloan at a moment when he was so obviously feeling his skills as a father were somehow lacking.

"All you can do," she hastily continued, pushing aside the dark feelings, "is the best you can do. And I know that's exactly what you're doing. It's all you've ever done."

He murmured his thanks. Then he asked, "But will it be enough? Will my best be enough to get my girls through these traumatic teen years?"

"It'll have to be," she told him. "It's all any parent has to offer...their best attempt. Besides, I think it'll be more traumatic for you than it will be for them. And I want you to remember, you're not alone in this, you know. You have me.''

Once again, the words she'd blurted out before taking the time to think left her feeling embarrassed beyond measure. She jerked to a standing position. This happened to her much too often when she was with this man. Much too often.

''I really should be getting back to work,'' she said, turning her back on him and making for the door.

''Rachel,'' he called.

She swiveled to face him, her head tilted to one side as she fought the wave of chagrin washing over her.

''What did you want?'' he asked. ''You did come in here to see me about something specific, didn't you?''

Her laugh sounded full of embarrassment even to her own ears. ''Of course I did. I can be so silly sometimes. I forgot. I wanted to tell you that Mrs. Lawrence still hasn't made a payment on her balance. It's been six months. Should I pass the account on to a collection agency?''

As if he didn't have enough to worry about, Rachel thought. She hated adding to his troubles at a time when he was already worried about his daughters. But it was office policy to discuss patient accounts with the doctors before she did anything as drastic as formally calling in a collection agency.

Sloan reached around and scrubbed at the back of his neck. ''No. We've collected some of the money from her insurance, haven't we?''

Rachel nodded. ''Eighty percent of the total bill.

That's the maximum her insurance will contribute. And that's for the test performed here in the office. They don't pay anything toward the actual office-visit fee. She owes a pretty substantial sum.''

He seemed to contemplate the situation for only a moment before saying, "Let's just forget about the balance for now. Mr. and Mrs. Lawrence are divorcing. Her son just joined the navy. She's having a tough time right now with her health. She doesn't need us breathing down her neck.''

He was such a good man, Rachel thought, closing the door of his office behind her. He didn't deserve to feel doubt over how he was raising his children. He didn't deserve to feel guilty that Olivia might not approve of his parenting abilities. He didn't deserve to have patients who wouldn't or couldn't pay for his time and expertise.

As she walked down the hallway, she sighed, her chest so full of heated emotion for the man she was afraid she couldn't contain it all.

Rachel stirred sugar into her cup of hot tea. She, Jane and Diana were at the mall, and the three of them were taking a short break from shopping to enjoy a slice of apple pie—the special of the day— and nice cup of English Breakfast tea in a small café.

She liked these ladies. Jane Hamilton, Greg's new wife, was a no-nonsense kind of person. What you saw was what you got. She was loving, caring. But Jane also spoke her mind, plainly, and Rachel respected that. Diana Chapman, Travis's fiancée, was contemplative and quiet, more reserved than Jane. However, Rachel quickly learned that, although Diana wasn't as quick to voice her opinion as Jane, the woman was utterly honest when she eventually did express her feelings and beliefs.

During their afternoon of shopping, their conversation had covered many different topics. As they relaxed in the café, they began discussing the results of some medical tests Jane had taken.

"When I was young," Jane explained, "I was hit by a car. The accident caused some internal damage. A small tear in my cervix. In itself, it wasn't much of a problem. But there was an infection which led to scar tissue. I was told that the scarring would prevent me from having children." Her smile was, at first, tentative, but in a heartbeat hope beamed from her like the rays of a glorious summer sun. "But Greg tells me that laser surgery could fix me right up."

"That's wonderful," Diana said.

"Yes," Rachel agreed.

Jane sobered. "I'm perfectly happy raising Joy. My niece has been a gift since the day she was born. She's the light of my life. Greg's, too." Her gaze clouded with a far away look. "But if I could have Greg's baby...a child of my own..." She sighed longingly.

Diana reached out and squeezed Jane's hand. "If it's meant to be, it will be. I'm sure of that."

Jane smiled a silent thank-you as she curled her finger through the handle of the delicate teacup.

"Kids," Rachel commented finally. "They can be both a blessing and a burden."

The three of them had already discussed the problems Sloan was having with his triplets, so when Rachel chuckled, Jane and Diana joined in, easily agreeing with her statement.

"But, you know," Jane said suddenly, "Sloan is so lucky to have you."

Rachel's hand stopped, poised in midair, the bite of pie on her fork momentarily forgotten. "That's a nice thing for you to say."

"It's the truth," she continued.

Glancing down at the tabletop, the woman obviously had more on her mind and was judging whether or not to express her thoughts. In true Jane fashion, she surrendered to the urge to voice her opinion.

"And further more," she said, her tone a hush, "I want you to know I'm rooting for you."

Bewilderment bit into Rachel's brow. Without even realizing it, she set down the fork. "Rooting for me?"

Jane nodded. "I've only been around all of you a couple of months, but...well, I can certainly see how you feel. About Sloan, I mean."

Rachel remained mute, unable to keep her eyes from blinking in surprise.

Diana's chuckle was effervescent. "A person would have to be a fool not to see it. And I wish you nothing but happiness."

A gasp rushed from Rachel's throat. "You, too?"

Diana nodded. Evidently realizing what she'd just said, Diana backpedaled by adding, "Not that I think Sloan is foolish, mind you."

"Of course not," Rachel said. Then she couldn't help but join in with Diana's infectious laughter. She'd been found out. By two women she'd thought were strangers. What she was learning was that Jane and Diana were quickly becoming her friends.

Her eyes suddenly prickling with warm emotion, Rachel dipped her head, sipped her tea and took a quick moment to gather her frayed wits.

When breast cancer had taken her best friend, Rachel had thought she'd never experience a female camaraderie as close as what she'd shared with Olivia. But here she was, feeling comfortable enough with Jane and Diana to actually consider talking about her feelings for Sloan.

She sighed. "I honestly believe nothing will ever come of what I feel for him," she found herself admitting. A great sadness fell over her, as heavy as a sodden blanket of snow.

"Like Diana said," Jane told Rachel, "Sloan isn't a fool. He'll come around. He'll notice how you feel."

Rachel couldn't seem to raise her gaze from the rim of her dessert plate.

Diana's hand on hers felt nice. It warmed her heart and had her lifting her chin to look at her newfound friends.

"It isn't just the problem of Sloan noticing, is it?" Diana asked. "You're battling your feelings for him. Suppressing them." Her voice softened as she asked, "Why would you do that?"

Astounded at Diana's intuitiveness, Rachel looked up. There were so many reasons why she shouldn't love Sloan. So many.

Finally, she quietly admitted, "I feel guilty." Inhaling deeply, she held the breath for an instant, then released it with a sigh. "I feel guilty that my best friend has died...and I'm in love with her husband. I want him." Again, hot unshed tears burned the backs of her eyelids. As difficult as it was, she forced herself to continue. "Not only do I want Olivia's husband, but I want her children. I love those girls. I want to be a permanent part of their lives."

Reaching up, she lightly swiped her fingertips across her forehead, down the length of her cheek. "I can't tell you how strange it is to finally hear myself admitting all this out loud. I've thought it, felt it, *dreamed* it for so long."

Tucking her hands into her lap, she dipped her chin low to her chest as she whispered, "I'm an awful person."

"You're no such thing," Jane exclaimed. "You're not hurting Olivia. You're not."

Rachel couldn't help but notice how quiet Diana had become. Collecting every bit of strength she could find, she looked across the table at the dark-haired Native American woman.

"What do you think, Diana?" Rachel asked. Her voice might sound tentative, but she was determined to seek an answer. "Am I terrible to want my best friend's life?"

Diana sat motionless for a moment or two. Finally, she said, "First of all, if you and Sloan were to get together, you wouldn't be stepping into Olivia's life. You're a different person. So is Sloan now. You can be assured that the things he's experienced have changed him. So your life will always be completely separate from the one she lived. The life you and Sloan might share would be very different than the one he shared with her."

The woman grew still again. Rachel waited patiently. Diana's pensive expression was evidence that she wasn't finished, and Rachel was terribly curious to hear more of her opinion.

Diana said, "I don't know what your spiritual beliefs are, but I have faith that once a person dies they become one with the Light of Understanding, the Light of Love. I believe that Olivia would want you to be happy. She would want Sloan to find someone with whom he could spend his life. And, more than anything else, she would want her children to be loved. Cared for."

If she had known these women better, Rachel might feel comfortable admitting the whole truth about Olivia. But seeing that her friendship with Jane and Diana was in its beginning stages, it just didn't seem right to try to explain her doubts or Olivia's complex nature.

She hoped all that Diana said was true. With all her heart, she did. The thought that Olivia was full of love and understanding, that she'd want only good things for everyone she'd left behind here on earth somehow made Rachel's heart buoyant.

All of a sudden, she found herself daring to look at her circumstances with a more optimistic eye.

Chapter Five

Never, in all the years that he'd been a single father, had Sloan found himself up to his elbows in flour. But that was exactly where he found himself now.

He'd left the office early this afternoon in order to pick up Sydney at her school and take her to the dentist to have a small cavity filled. On the way home, his daughter had reminded him that the school's winter fair was the next day. This Saturday event was a huge fund-raiser meant to accumulate money that would be used for new books in the school's library.

"I need six dozen cookies for the bake sale," she'd told him.

His first thought was to reprimand Sydney for waiting until the last minute to tell him about the cookies. However, he tried to be understanding and he'd forced himself to remain calm, assuring her they could tackle this problem. It being too late to place an order at the bakery, the two of them had stopped at the local supermarket and purchased flour, sugar, vanilla, butter, eggs and chocolate chips. Surely he could whip up six dozen cookies in a couple of hours. Especially with help from the three girls.

They could do this, he'd been sure as he packed the grocery sacks into the trunk of the car. And he'd felt they just might have some good old-fashioned father-daughter fun while they baked together.

However, now he found himself all alone in the kitchen mumbling under his breath as he studied Betty Crocker's recipe for chocolate-chip cookies.

Upon arriving home, however, Sydney had marched into the house and promptly declared that she couldn't possibly help with the baking. She had not one, but three posters to make for the fair. Mrs. Dalley would be furious if the posters weren't ready, she'd said. Besides, Sydney revealed, she had a long-term project that was due on Monday and she simply had to work on her essay.

Sloan had grumbled then, and he hadn't felt the least bit guilty when he'd snapped at Sydney to go to her room and get to work.

Children. They could drive a man right up the wall.

He measured a second cup of flour into the butter, sugar and eggs he'd creamed together in the large mixing bowl as the cookbook had instructed. A teaspoon of salt. A teaspoon of baking powder and soda. A teaspoon of vanilla. But when he picked up the spoon to stir the conglomeration, a cloud of the white floury mixture somehow puffed into the air, dusting his forearms and trousers with a gritty coating.

Sighing, he set down the spoon and reached for the dish towel.

Rachel was on her way from the office with Sophie and Sasha. As soon as the girls arrived he'd let his two remaining daughters take over. Sydney might have made other commitments, but the other girls would surely be happy to pitch in.

It was good of Rachel to help him when he found himself in a pinch like today. With Sydney's dental appointment, he'd been unable to be at the office, where the school bus normally let the girls off each afternoon. Normal routine had the triplets sitting in the conference room doing their homework until he finished up with his last patient, and then they would all come home together. He didn't like the idea of the girls being home alone after school. But on days when he couldn't be at the office, Rachel always offered to tend the girls and then bring them home once the office closed.

On the rare occasions when this situation arose, Rachel would nearly always go one step further and pick up something for their dinner. And he hoped to high heaven she'd done just that today, as he didn't think he would find the time to fix a meal. As she trooped in with Sophie and Sasha, Rachel was carrying white containers of Chinese take-out, and he couldn't help smiling as he thought she had once again come through with flying colors.

Heat churned low in his belly at the sight of her. He did his best to ignore the reaction as the kitchen filled with a flurry of activity. The girls flung off their coats, hanging them on the coatrack by the kitchen door, and stowed their book-filled backpacks while Sloan gathered dishes and cutlery to set the table for dinner. On nights such as these, Rachel always stayed to eat with them. However, since their intimate encounter on the dance floor on New Year's Eve, their relationship had become very awkward even though she'd made a point to tell him that the kiss meant absolutely nothing. Well, it might have meant nothing to her, but that kiss had not only rocked him to the core, it had stirred something inside him. Something *deep* inside him. And he seemed to be seeing Rachel in a whole new light.

Hesitantly, he asked, "You, uh, are planning to stay? For dinner, I mean."

"Jeez, Dad," Sasha said. "Rachel always stays for dinner when she brings us home."

Rachel tossed him a tentative smile and a quick nod, and then she began opening the cartons of Chinese food.

"Did Sydney make out okay at the dentist?" she asked.

He nodded. "The cavity was so small she didn't need to be numbed up."

"Good. I know she doesn't like needles."

"Who does?" Sophie asked. She plopped herself down in a chair.

Sloan narrowed his eyes at his daughter. "How about getting some napkins? And fill some glasses with ice."

With eyes rolling, she sighed and did as he said.

"I'll go get Sydney," Sasha offered, slipping out of the room.

"So what are you up to?" Rachel asked him, eyeing the baking ingredients, bowls and utensils sitting on the counter.

Sloan sighed heavily. "The school's Winter Fair is tomorrow. Sydney told me she needed six dozen cookies for the bake table."

"Oh, yeah," Sophie said as she opened the freezer for ice, "I need cookies, too."

He frowned. "What do you mean, *too?*"

Sophie shrugged. "I need cookies. Six dozen."

Rachel and Sloan went still, dreadful insight striking them simultaneously as their gazes locked together.

"Sasha!" he yelled.

The daughter in question was just returning to the kitchen with Sydney.

"What did I do?" Sasha said.

Ignoring her question, Sloan asked one of his own. "Do you need cookies for the fair tomorrow?"

"Only six dozen."

Sloan sank down into a chair. "How are we going to bake eighteen dozen cookies in one night?"

Sophie carried two glasses over to the table. "We? Sasha and I can't help with the baking. We were assigned to make the welcome banner for the fair tomorrow."

"And don't forget," Sasha added, "we have a—"

"I know," Sloan said, unable to keep the defeat from his tone, "you both have essays that are due on Monday."

Sasha nodded.

"I'll help," Rachel quickly replied.

"Oh, I can't ask you to give up a Friday night," Sloan said.

"Don't be silly." She stuck a serving spoon in the carton containing steamed rice.

His mind began churning. Maybe the two of them could pull this off. "But I don't think I have enough ingredients for—"

"After we eat, I'll run out to the store while you work on that batch you've started," Rachel offered. "Don't worry. We can pull this off."

Sloan smiled to hear her voicing his exact thoughts. She was a wonder, Rachel was, and he felt the tension in his shoulders begin to subside.

As the hours wore on while they measured, stirred and baked in the kitchen, Sloan learned something about Rachel. Her organizational skills didn't stop at efficiently managing an office. She'd have made a great administrator in any kitchen in the world, as well. She'd insisted that they clean up as they went, so the counters and sink never became cluttered with dirty bowls and utensils. And she'd quickly pointed out that doubling each batch would cut down on mixing time, if nothing else.

Early in the evening when the first cookies had come out of the oven, warm and soft, the smell of rich chocolate wafting on the air, Rachel had narrowed her eyes and warned him he would be risking a couple of broken fingers if he touched even one. He'd laughed at her, but promised to wrestle down his urge to taste until the two hundred sixteenth cookie had been lifted onto the cooling rack. Only then would he indulge his sweet tooth.

Tasting a cookie wasn't the only urge he was fighting. The desire to taste Rachel's luscious lips was a craving that nearly bested him, time and again. But he continued to beat it back.

He watched her slide the spatula under a cookie and shift it to the rectangular cooling rack. The soft light overhead glistened on her full bottom lip. Forcing himself to look away, he focused his attention on boxing up the cooled baked goods.

He guessed this most sensual torment was caused by the fact that she'd rescued him, yet again, from what had seemed to him a dire situation. But then he frowned, nearly shaking his head, as another part of his mind silently argued with that logic.

She'd come to his aid more times than he could count over the years. Especially since Sloan had found himself a single man raising his girls alone. Why would his attraction to Rachel wait until now to rear up?

"What's wrong?" she asked him. "Your frown is deeper than that snowdrift by the back door."

"Nothing." His quick answer sounded as if it had been muttered under his breath.

Great. What he didn't need right now was her questioning him about the agony of desiring her— the agony he was attempting to hide.

"I'm just having a bit of trouble getting the cookies to fit in the box," he lied.

That sexy mouth of yours is tormenting me nearly to death. The truth of the matter echoed through his brain. No, he quickly decided, he couldn't acknowledge that. Somehow, he doubted she'd understand.

He almost chuckled at his outrageous thoughts. The small lie was easier. And safer.

"Well, don't crowd them," she warned. "We don't want them to arrive in pieces. That would defeat the purpose of all this effort we're making."

She was so serious. Humor curled the corners of his mouth. "We sure don't want that."

"We'd be the laughingstock of the Winter Fair," she said, seeming not to notice the amusement that had touched his response.

I'll tell you what I do want.... The thought exploded from the back of his mind like a short-fused bomb. *You.* Oddly, the idea struck him in two areas at once—deep down in his gut where heat curled deliciously, and directly in the funny bone.

The combination resulted in a strange sensation. He pressed his lips together, but the comical urge broke through in the form of a soft chuckle.

"First you're frowning," she commented, turning her head to gaze at him curiously, "now you're laughing. What's up with you?"

"I haven't a clue." He realized this was the honest truth. "I'm sure it's just that I'm tired."

That was the culprit, he realized. Fatigue. He'd been on his feet at the office all day, and he'd been busy in this kitchen all night. It was nearly eleven o'clock, and the alarm had gotten him out of bed at six this morning. He was bone weary.

Exhaustion was making him eye Rachel's mouth like it was a succulent confection and he a starving man.

Fatigue, indeed, the voice in his head silently

chided him. *You go ahead and think what you like. Go on deceiving yourself if you like.*

"And there you go," Rachel said lightly, "frowning again." She sighed. "What we need is to go to bed. The both of us."

He knew full well she hadn't meant the remark to be in any way suggestive, but he was helpless against the impulse to capitalize on her statement, and to offer her a lopsided, mischievous grin.

"You've got my vote."

The unmistakable insinuation in his words had her gaze snapping up to meet his. The silky tone of his voice surprised even him.

The air in the room changed with that one small remark.

It was as if the molecules in the atmosphere speeded up, and so did his heart rate. Not to mention how his temperature escalated. He felt the need to reach up and tug at the collar of his sweater.

And he wasn't the only one who felt the change. Rachel's delectable mouth curled into a slow and quizzical smile.

"Why, Sloan Radcliff," she quietly said. "If I didn't know you so well, I'd say you were teasing me."

His grin widened. One shoulder lifted in a shrug. His brows rose a fraction, too. "Maybe you don't know me as well as you think."

He didn't know himself, that was for certain. He had no idea what had gotten into him, but minute bolts of lightning seemed to snap and spark around them and he liked this feeling. This very playful, very...*sensuous* feeling.

Her honey-colored eyes twinkled as she softly replied, "Maybe I don't."

Low laughter rumbled up from deep in his chest. "I'm glad to know I'm not as staid and predictable as everyone thinks." He captured her with his gaze. "It's great to know I can surprise you after all the years we've known each other."

As he spoke, something—magnetism, attraction, lust—propelled him forward. He inched closer to her. And closer still, until their noses nearly touched.

"*Staid* is a word I'd never have used to describe you," she said in a hushed voice. "But I will admit you have been awfully unpredictable lately."

Her dark gaze seemed filled with amazement at what was happening, and her lips were parted in what he deliberately decided to take as an invitation.

Inviting him to kiss her was probably far from her mind. Most likely, in her total shock and amazement, she was pondering which lunatic asylum to commit him to.

He didn't mind. He wanted to go crazy. He wanted to spend this one moment reveling in complete insanity. He didn't want to think about his impending actions. He only wanted to act.

Dipping his head, he let his mouth whisper against hers. It couldn't have been described as a kiss really, just a caressing brush of skin against skin. He felt the cool rush of her breath as she gasped a quick, short inhalation.

Clearly, she was astonished by his behavior. Well…she wasn't alone in that. However, the realization didn't cause him to abandon his quest.

Leaning into her, aware of the heat of her thighs

against his, the firmness of her tummy pressed against him, the pressure of her breasts against his chest, he tenderly took her bottom lip between his teeth. All kinds of sensations coursed through his body. His pulse thrummed. His blood raced.

On his tongue, he tasted a buttery sweetness. And chocolate.

He pulled back just enough to look into her eyes. "You ate a cookie."

Instant remorse flickered in her gaze, and a tiny frown creased the small area between her eyes. Sloan thought the expression was as sexy as hell.

"Just a nibble," she finally admitted. "When you went up to check that the girls had gone to bed."

He could no more have stopped his laughter than he could have stopped the moon from orbiting the earth, or the stars from twinkling like gems in the clear winter sky.

"But you threatened to beat me if I ate one."

Her face tightened with contrition. "I didn't actually threaten to *beat* you...."

"You didn't," he agreed with a small nod. "Actually, you threatened to break my bones."

Her expression constricted even more. "I did, didn't I?"

She looked utterly contrite. And as cute as could be. Desire welled up in Sloan as it never had before in his entire life.

"You know what the rule book says about bad girls, don't you?"

The fear she feigned made her golden-brown eyes grow round. "What does the rule book say?" she breathed.

"They get punished," he replied, oh so softly.
"With kisses."

"Oh, my."

Something mysterious lit her gaze. Something
earthy. Raw.

Seconds simmered. Hesitation hummed on the
outer edges of his consciousness, but he refused it
entrance, shut it out completely, in fact.

She reached up to slide her fingers into his hair.

"So...quit torturing me—" her tone exuded a
fluid and stunningly palpable sensuality "—and give
me the punishment I'm due."

Finally, their mouths met.

Moonlight glistened on the snow-covered trees in
the cold, clear night. Rachel shivered where she sat
in the window seat in her bedroom. But she didn't
move to retrieve the blanket from the bed...the blanket that would so easily and thoroughly offer her
warmth and comfort.

If there was one thing she didn't deserve right
now, it was warmth and comfort. She deserved all
the discomfort that the night chill could wreak on
her; gooseflesh, chattering teeth, muscle stiffness.
She'd earned all that and more.

Winter's nip wasn't the only thing plaguing her.
The guilt she felt was more sharp and stinging, more
skin-numbing, than the crisp draft coming through
the old, single-paned window.

How could she have flirted with Sloan so bra-
zenly?

He'd been exhausted. He'd said as much. That's
why he'd teased the way he had. That heated kiss

they had shared hadn't been his fault. She should have put a stop to his antics. She'd been alert. Not tired in the least. When he'd begun getting silly... when he'd started teasing and flirting...she should have called a halt.

But she hadn't. In fact, she'd done the unthinkable. She'd joined in.

Why, she'd practically pulled the man's face to hers, shouting, "Stop torturing me and kiss me already!"

Well, maybe she hadn't shouted, but she'd asked for what had happened. Begged for it, really. Rachel sighed. And she shivered. But, still, she didn't reach for the blanket.

"I'm sorry, Olivia," she whispered out toward the window, hoping her words would be carried to heaven so that her friend could hear them.

Guilt rolled over her and hot tears blurred her vision, fragmenting the night scene into slivers glistening with reflected moonlight.

"I'm so sorry."

Rachel felt like a tart, a floozy. All manner of wicked names floated through her mind.

Normally, she'd have laughed, remembering the mean, juvenile terms that Olivia had breezily flung at anyone who displeased her when the two of them had been teenaged best friends. But Rachel didn't laugh now. She didn't even smile.

The advice Diana had given her on their shopping trip had been wonderful. And Rachel had even allowed herself to go so far as to consider that it might be true. However, the idea that Olivia would want Rachel and Sloan to be happy *together*—well, that just wasn't conceivable to Rachel. Olivia had put too much effort into maneuvering, plotting and manipulating her relationship with Sloan to see him end up with anyone else.

*Any*one else.

Too easily, Rachel envisioned her friend pointing the finger of blame, narrowing angry eyes, shouting terrible names.

Tart. Floozy.

And Rachel felt as if those descriptions fit her to a T. The worst thing about it was…she knew in her heart that Olivia wouldn't have hesitated to agree.

"How come you're not parking the car?" Sophie asked, confusion knitting her brow.

Sasha chimed, "You aren't coming inside?"

"You've got to come to the fair, Dad," Sydney said. "What will the teachers think if you don't make an appearance?"

"Don't you mean 'what will they think if I don't show up to spend some money'?"

Tired and out-of-sorts, Sloan knew full well that the comment was out of line. However, rather than retracting the statement, he only gripped the steering wheel tighter and heaved a sigh.

Yesterday had been hard on him, what with working at the office all day, running his daughter to the dentist and then to the store, slaving over those cookies into the wee hours…and being plagued by those erotic dreams of Rachel hadn't helped matters at all. In fact, the imaginary kisses and phantom caresses had been sheer torture. He'd awakened feeling just as tired as when he'd fallen into bed around one this morning.

But his biggest tormentor was his own guilt. It sat on his shoulders, sharp and heavy, like a stack of granite shards.

What on earth had possessed him to dally with Rachel in such an outrageous manner? He'd completely taken leave of his senses.

What would the girls think if they knew? What would everyone think?

What would Olivia think?

The question caused hot, searing pains of anguish to shoot through him, stab at him. Anguish beyond belief.

Yes, sensuous dreams of Rachel had beleaguered him through the night. But it was the burdensome guilt that weighed him down to a nearly overwhelming degree. If he didn't do something to make amends, he wouldn't be able to shake the gloomy cloud that hovered over him.

"There's someplace I have to go," he told his daughters. "Something I have to do. I won't be long. I'll be back in forty-five minutes. An hour, tops. Then I'll buy back all those cookies Rachel and I baked. Well, some of them, anyway."

As the triplets scrambled out of the car, he said, "Don't forget those cookies," even though he knew they wouldn't.

"Got 'em right here." Sydney lifted up her neatly packed box.

The other girls did the same.

Sasha turned back toward the car. "Rachel said

she was coming. Did she tell you when she'd get here?''

At the mention of the woman's name, a strange and exciting electricity ricocheted through him—and at the same time, the dark guilt twisted in his gut like the wrenching of a sharp knife.

''I don't know when she plans to come,'' he told his daughter. ''But if she said she'd be here, she'll be here.''

Sasha nodded. ''You're right. Rachel never disappoints us.''

Forcing a smile onto his lips, he responded, ''She sure doesn't.''

Chapter Six

The florist had charged a bundle for the bouquet of pristine white roses. But Sloan didn't mind, really. It was the middle of winter, and perfect blooms were even more costly than usual off-season. The assault on his wallet was just one more part of his penance. Besides, roses were her favorite. And bringing them as an offering might help to ease—if not the tremendous guilt he suffered—at least, his mind.

The cemetery was bleak at any time of year, but it was especially so during January. Trees were bare, the grass dry and dormant, and the Pennsylvania wildlife had either flown south to warmer climes or remained huddled in their nests and burrows trying to keep warm. Barren and gray, the graveyard offered no solace whatsoever.

Not that he had expected any.

He was simply answering a call. An incessant and haunting call.

Without warning, Sloan's memory catapulted him back to the day he'd buried his wife. The sky had been bright with sunshine, the summer's heat beating down on the family and friends who had attended Olivia's funeral.

His girls had been little troupers through the whole ordeal. They had kept their chins up—for his sake, he'd been sure—shedding tears neither at the funeral home nor the cemetery where they had driven in a long caravan to lay their mother to rest.

Oh, it wasn't as if they hadn't cried at all. They had wept plenty during the months when the cancer had slowly but surely made Olivia weaker and weaker, sicker and sicker. No measure had stopped the tumors from forming…and growing. Not surgery. Not chemotherapy. Not radiation. Nothing.

Black guilt wrapped itself around his neck like a predatory snake, strangling, choking. Clearing his throat in the silence of the car, he gripped the steering wheel with hands that now shook as the tires slowly rolled over the cemetery's gravel road.

How could he call himself a doctor, a healer of the sick, and not have noticed that his own wife had been dying before his very eyes? For weeks, she'd been ill, and he hadn't been aware of it. For all he knew, the cancer that had finally metastasized throughout her entire body could have been attacking her for months, and all that time he'd been concentrating all his attention on his budding medical practice and his new patients.

Self-reproach, slimy and reptilian, constricted tighter around his throat. He had to actually part his lips and concentrate on dragging in one breath, and then another. Mentally, he resisted the blame he felt—would *always* feel—and tried to focus on his previous thought: how his little girls had handled themselves the day of their mother's funeral.

Sloan knew they had made some sort of sisterly pact to remain dry-eyed. And it hadn't been easy for the then ten-year-olds. He'd urged them to cry, but each time he had, they had only hugged him around the waist or wrapped their small hands around his and given him a warm squeeze.

He'd come to the conclusion that they must have emptied themselves of tears over the weeks and months that Olivia had been in the hospital. Not to mention the night before the funeral, when all four of them had huddled together on the living-room carpet and bawled like orphaned babes.

Something had happened that night, a closeness between them had been sparked. A devotion he had never before experienced with his daughters. And that affection they had found had made the grieving process just a little bit easier for them all, he'd felt.

As he thought about Sasha, Sydney and Sophie now, and the estrangement he so often felt from them of late, Sloan wondered where that wonderful closeness had gone, where that deep affection they had experienced after Olivia's death might be hiding…and how he might once again conjure it.

Just then, he drove up over the last rise that would lead him to Olivia's grave site and was surprised to see Rachel's car parked off to the side of the road. He pulled in behind her car, cut the engine and reached for the roses he'd bought for Olivia.

A soft smile curved his lips as he exited from the

car's warmth into the chill of the morning. He had known that Rachel used to make weekly visits to the cemetery…she'd even brought the girls any Saturday that they wished to go. But he hadn't realized her visits had continued all this time.

Tugging the zipper of his leather coat to his chin, he tucked his head into the slight but cool breeze and headed over the grassy slope.

He stopped a few feet away, and just watched her standing there by the grave. She didn't turn, and he suspected that because the light wind blew toward him, she hadn't even heard him approaching. He should call out to her. But he simply stood there gazing at her, wondering about the odd hitch he felt in his chest at the sight of her flaming hair, her long, shapely body that even her forest-green wool coat couldn't hide.

The sound of her voice surprised him. Maybe she had spied him, after all.

However, he quickly realized she was speaking, not to him but to Olivia.

"So," Rachel said into the frosty air, "I want you to know that I'm sorry. I'm so very, very sorry."

He frowned and his heart twisted painfully. Why on earth was Rachel apologizing? But before his brain could even begin to find an answer, something in the tone of her voice touched him. Hell, touched him didn't quite describe what happened to his gut. Something in her tone rocked him to the very core of his being.

He'd come here to apologize, himself. Guilt was the foundation of what had driven him. He knew that. And it bothered him greatly to think that Rachel suffered with feeling to blame for anything. Anything at all.

Confusion mounted in him as he hoped she'd say more. Yes, he was eavesdropping. And he probably shouldn't be. But he simply had to know what it was that had her asking for Olivia's forgiveness.

Finally, she spoke again. "I know now that, no matter what I might be feeling, I shouldn't have kissed him."

Ah. So she, too, was feeling guilty over the closeness they had shared in the kitchen last night. Not all of her statement made sense to him—and a little voice in the back of his mind urged him to ponder her words further—but he understood enough now to realize that Rachel was standing over Olivia's grave to express regret.

Compassion welled up in him, hot and fierce. Before he had time to think a single thought, his feet were propelling him forward.

"Rachel," he said.

The surprise on her beautiful face almost made him smile.

"I couldn't help but overhear your apology," he continued. "You have nothing to be sorry for. Absolutely nothing. I'm at fault. I take full responsibility. You don't owe Olivia an apology."

She looked stricken. Her dark eyes darted away from his. It was clear she didn't believe a word he'd said.

Reaching out, he grasped the sleeve of her coat between cold fingers. "I mean it, Rachel. You were innocent in…well, in what happened between us last night."

Instead of looking at him, she dipped her chin lower.

He held up the bouquet. "You see, I felt guilty, too. I came to make amends."

"White roses were her favorite."

Rachel's voice was a mere whisper. Still, she didn't look him in the eye.

He nodded, even though he knew Rachel wasn't aware of the movement. "I thought a quick visit out here might make me feel better." He bent down and placed the flowers at the base of the pink granite headstone. Quickly, he stood and faced Rachel again. "But I need you to know that you aren't to blame. That kiss was one-hundred-percent my fault. Do you hear me?"

It took a few seconds of silence, but finally she lifted her gaze to his.

His brows rose at the sight of her face. Before she had a chance to speak a single word, he said, "Your nose is as red as a hothouse poppy." He slid his fingers along her jaw. "And your cheeks are like ice. How long have you been out here?"

Without waiting for an answer, he wrapped his arm around her and propelled her back toward their cars.

"We need to get some hot coffee into you."

"But what about the fair?" she asked weakly. "The girls? I told them I'd—"

"Don't worry," he replied. "The girls are safe and they're having a ball at the school. They've got plenty of supervision, and I told them I'd be there soon. We can certainly sit over a cup of coffee for twenty minutes while you get warm."

"I am a little chilly," she admitted.

"I'd say you're frozen to the bone."

He'd come here to make a speech to Olivia, to admit that he was a heel, a jerk, a louse. However, all he'd done was toss down the flowers and walk away. He should feel horrible. But, somehow, taking care of Rachel seemed more important at the moment.

Appeasing his self-reproach could wait. Past experience told him the guilt that plagued him would return soon enough. It always did.

Rachel silently watched the waitress pour steaming coffee into the utilitarian white cups sitting on the table between herself and Sloan. She was unable to make her gaze lift to his face. She was mortified by their meeting in the cemetery.

He'd come upon her just as she was explaining herself to Olivia…trying in vain to somehow justify her actions.

What on earth had possessed her to actually speak out loud for all the world to hear? It wasn't as if Olivia was actually there, perched on her tombstone, or hovering over it. Rachel knew full well that her deceased friend was unable to perceive sound…or offer forgiveness. So why had she been so foolish as to go there seeking pardon, baring her soul in such a…well, in such a *verbal* manner?

From Sloan's response, it seemed that he'd only heard the very last of her speech, the part where she'd voiced regret over kissing him. However, if he'd arrived at Olivia's grave just two seconds earlier, he'd have heard every word—the whole wretched confession. However, just because he hadn't mentioned it didn't mean he hadn't heard. The poor man might be too shocked to comment on what he'd learned from her lamentation.

Standing there among the rows of headstones, Rachel had finally admitted everything that was in her heart. To herself. To Olivia. To the clouds and the trees and the grass and the wind. And maybe even to Sloan. A horrified shiver coursed through her at the thought.

She'd worked up to it, of course. First, she'd expressed her deep love for Olivia's daughters. Then she'd ventured into dangerous territory by suggesting that the triplets needed a mother figure in their lives and admitting her desire to be more to the girls than merely a concerned family friend. Then she'd dived in over her head when she'd blurted out her overwhelming attraction to Sloan. And, finally, her desperate love for him—a love that she'd been trying to hide from everyone, herself included, for years.

Describing the kiss she and Sloan had shared in the kitchen last night had been agony for her, because it had rekindled all the heat and passion and need she'd felt. But remaining silent about it had been utterly impossible. Had she been somehow trying to convince Olivia that she'd be good for Sloan? That he deserved some happiness? Or had she been trying to convince *herself* of these things? To justify her behavior. And her feelings. Self-reproach and condemnation had attacked her as she stood by her friend's grave. And the deep sorrow and regret swamping her had culminated in the gravesite finale: her heartfelt apology. For everything. Her selfishness where Sophie, Sydney and Sasha were concerned. Her greedy desire for Sloan. Even the reckless kiss the two of them had shared.

And that's when Sloan had made his presence known.

She'd stifled the shocked gasp that had started to rush from her when she'd heard him call out her name. But she knew she hadn't succeeded in totally hiding her surprise. Immediately she'd experienced a knee-quaking trepidation over how much of her revealing soliloquy he might have overheard. However, up to now all he'd commented on was the blame she'd placed on herself. The blame over their kiss. He'd refused to allow her to take responsibility for what had happened between them.

Slanting a quick glance at his face, she surreptitiously watched him stir his coffee, and her heart warmed. It was so nice of him to try to put her mind at ease.

Hopefully, she had nothing to worry about. Hopefully, he hadn't overheard her full confession. If he'd discovered her true feelings for him, surely he'd fess up, wouldn't he?

"I have a confession to make."

Her eyes widened in silent alarm, her gaze riveted on his handsome face. The statement he'd made parroted her own thoughts to the point that her mouth nearly dropped open. Her heart hammered against her ribs.

But his attention was firmly fixed on the rim of the cup he now clasped between his hands. How would he react to knowing her feelings for him?

Anxiety gnawed at her nerves like a herd of starving mice.

He sighed, not lifting his eyes. "That kiss we shared isn't the only thing I'm to blame for."

The utter misery in his tone made her frown. The wave of sympathy that welled up in her completely drowned all the anxiety she'd experienced only a second before. All that was left in its wake was empathy and concern for Sloan. No one should be made to feel as despondent as he looked at this moment.

Several questions spun through her head, but she remained silent, quite sure that he'd eventually expand on his statement.

For what seemed an interminable length of time, he remained motionless and mute. When he finally did speak, his voice was a rusty whisper.

"I let her die, Rachel."

He didn't have to reveal of whom he was speaking. Even a blithering fool would have known he meant Olivia.

She wanted to reach out to him, to squeeze his forearm comfortingly, to croon words of assurance, argue that he was terribly wrong to think such a thing about himself. But something in his expression stopped her from acting on those urges. Never in her life had she seen him like this.

Sure, she'd witnessed him at his weakest. She'd been there when he'd been trapped in the throes of despair, in the deepest depths of grief, when Olivia had passed away. But even through his grief, he'd been strong for his girls. This was different. He looked…brittle. Almost fragile. And Rachel couldn't help thinking that, if she were to touch him, he just might shatter like an antique looking glass, into a thousand soul-splintering shards.

"If I'm such a good doctor," he blurted out the vicious whisper, "why in the hell couldn't I save the life of my own wife?"

He didn't expect an answer. She knew that. She also realized that the brutal tone was directed, not at her, but at himself.

"You're not a cancer specialist," she gently pointed.

"You think that matters?"

Coming from anyone else, at any other time, the harshness of the question would have hurt her. But in her heart, she knew Sloan meant her no harm. Guilt was spurring him. Deeply felt and terribly personal. It was obviously a burden he'd been carrying around for a long time.

In that instant, Rachel realized something. For years she'd suffered with the knowledge that she had wronged her best friend by having fallen in love with Sloan. The guilt of that idea had weighed heavily on her, more so recently than ever before. But compared to the devastating self-reproach Sloan was now exhibiting, Rachel's guilt was nothing. It was as light as a silk shawl in comparison to the bulky, wet, woolen shroud Sloan was hauling around on his shoulders.

"Yes," she said, nodding. "I do think it matters. You're making it sound as though you had a hand in seeing to it Olivia came down with breast cancer."

It was a ridiculous notion, and she'd only said it as an attempt to shock him into realizing that the idea that he'd somehow allowed his wife to die was just as absurd.

"I should have caught it earlier," he said. "I should have realized she was ill. I should have noticed the signs."

"There were no signs for you to notice. She was the only one who could have noticed the signs. But she didn't. There is no blame to be placed here."

"I should have reminded her to perform monthly breast exams on herself. I should have—"

"Sloan, her gynecologist reminded her to examine her breasts," Rachel said. "Every gynecologist in this country reminds women that self-examination is the best form of early detection, you know that. Just as women over forty are urged to have yearly mammograms. Why are you beating yourself up about this?"

Angry fire sparked in his dark eyes.

"Because I deserve to be beaten up," he told her. "I deserve to have the tar kicked out of me."

Then, in an instant, something strange happened. His anger turned to full-fledged fury. Rachel could see it building and building, although the time that elapsed couldn't have been more than a heartbeat, maybe two.

Finally, his agony evidently became more than he could contain and he blurted out, "I didn't love her enough, damn it! I didn't care enough about her to keep her from getting sick. *To keep her from dying.*"

He lifted one hand, resting his elbow on the tabletop, and scoured at his forehead with his fingertips. His anger seemed to fade with the huge sigh he exhaled. When next he looked at her, Rachel saw resignation in his brown gaze. Somehow, the acceptance he so obviously felt was more disturbing to her than the powerful, self-directed anger and guilt she had just seen.

Touched by a tremendous sadness, she tucked her top lip between her teeth and bit down in an attempt to keep her emotional tears at bay. It was clear that this was a belief he felt he'd have to live with for the rest of his life. That gloomy thought over-whelmed her.

She inhaled around the lump in her throat. Willed her emotions under control.

Her voice was feather-soft as she said, "No matter how much you loved Olivia, you couldn't have saved her, Sloan. Everyone tried. The specialists. You. The nurses. The girls. Even me. We all tried. A lot of people loved her. Cared about her. We just couldn't save her."

"But...you don't understand."

His desolation was unmistakable. Finally, she could hold off her urge to comfort him no longer. Reaching out, she slid her fingertips over the corded muscle of his forearm. She felt the heat of his body radiating through the cotton shirt that stood between his skin and hers.

"Then make me understand," she quietly pleaded.

He cleared his throat with difficulty, wretched despair plain in his dark eyes.

"What, Sloan?" she asked. "What is it?"

For a moment, he pressed his lips together and she thought he'd decided not to confide in her. But he had to. Whatever was tormenting him had to come out into the open. Had to be dealt with.

His inhalation was shaky. His eyes lifted to hers.

"I didn't love her." His dark head shook as he said the words. "Not like a man should love his wife. Not like a man should love the mother of his children. I cared about her. And I certainly didn't want the cancer to take her life…but…"

The tension in Rachel's shoulders made her muscles begin to ache. She frowned, and now it was her head that was shaking in total bewilderment.

"I don't understand what you're saying." Unwittingly, Rachel's hand slid away from his arm, but her eyes never lost contact with his. "Of course you cared about her. You loved her. You married her. The two of you had a family together. You had a home."

The two of you had all the things I've always wanted. The thought whispered through her head like a specter. Echoing. Haunting.

It should have been odd, arguing with Sloan about whether or not he had loved his wife. Rachel's emotions for him ran so deep, she should have *wanted* to hear that he hadn't loved Olivia. But, as complicated as it seemed, that wasn't the case at all. Rachel had cared a great deal about her best friend. She wanted nothing more than to know that Olivia had been loved by her husband while she'd been alive.

Rachel wasn't stupid. She had realized early on that Olivia and Sloan hadn't shared the perfect relationship. It would have been impossible to have been Olivia's friend and not have known about the tricks the woman had pulled, the lies she'd told. However, Rachel had never thought for a minute that

Sloan hadn't been happy in the union he'd shared with Olivia.

She didn't know what she expected from him. To renounce what he'd said about not loving Olivia? To admit it was all a mistake? To say that of course he and Olivia had been utterly blissful while they'd been married?

The creases biting into her brow deepened as realization slowly sank into her brain. He'd meant what he'd said. And he had no intention of recanting his statement.

She moistened her paper-dry lips. Quietly, she asked, "What do you mean, you didn't love her?"

He cast his gaze to some far corner of the room, as if he couldn't quite bear to look at her as he confessed to this awful sin.

His shoulders lifted in an unconscious shrug as he explained, "I didn't love her." He heaved a sigh. "Just before we married, I had it in my mind to break things off with Olivia. I'd gone so far as to tell her I wasn't happy. I probably should have just ended it. I shouldn't have brought the subject up for discussion. It wasn't as if there was anything she could have done. I simply...wasn't happy being with her."

"But you married her."

"I didn't really have a choice," he pointed out. "She'd become pregnant."

"Y-you were sleeping with her."

Rachel didn't mean for her blurted retorts to sound like accusations. She wasn't an innocent. She knew that randy young college men slept with women they didn't love all the time. But for some reason, Sloan didn't seem to fit that description. If Olivia had become pregnant by Sloan, then the two of them had been in love.

"Not at the end I wasn't." His tone was a mere murmur. "Not for weeks and weeks. Not while I was trying to end our relationship."

The news stunned Rachel. Stunned her into complete silence.

He sat back against the booth seat. "I was shocked when she came to me and said she was pregnant."

With her mind in chaos, Rachel picked up the thick china cup and brought it to her lips. The coffee had grown tepid, tasted nasty on her tongue. But she swallowed it anyway.

Discovering that Olivia's web of lies and deception had entangled not only Sloan but herself as well was overwhelming for Rachel. Words wouldn't form in her head. Thoughts refused to solidify.

"Olivia was quick to get her parents and mine involved in the decision-making," Sloan continued. "Of course, everyone thought the right thing was for us to marry." He shrugged. "Since Olivia was having my child...we didn't know at the time that she was going to have triplets...I did the only thing I could. I did the *right* thing. I abandoned my plans of becoming a doctor. I quit college and married her."

But Olivia wasn't pregnant when you married her.

The thought rose in her throat like bitter bile, but thank the good Lord in heaven, Rachel was able to keep the truth from rolling off her tongue.

The school's winter festival was a blur to Rachel. As usual, Sloan's girls were three bundles of energy, eager to introduce Rachel to everyone they met. Rachel bought oodles of crafts and baked goods and, as she made each purchase, patiently listened to teachers and students alike explain how the profits would be used to buy books for the school library.

At the end of the day, the triplets had begged their father to allow them to go home with Rachel. However, he'd sternly pointed out that they were currently grounded, due to their antics at school. Then he'd reminded them that the garage was waiting to be cleaned and organized, as well as their closets. They had rolled their eyes and groaned at the unfairness of it all as only preteens could, but they didn't argue further with their father.

Rachel had been relieved, actually, that Sloan hadn't allowed the girls to come home with her. She loved them, enjoyed them immensely. But she needed some time alone to digest all the things that Sloan had told her this morning.

So here she sat in her apartment, over a cup of tea she'd already reheated twice due to the fact that she kept getting lost in the past.

Olivia had been a complicated person. A woman so full of need that she had done things normal people wouldn't even have considered doing.

When Rachel had first met Olivia, she'd thought it amazing that someone coming from such an affluent background, someone who seemed to have it all, could be so empty inside. Olivia seemed desperate to be loved.

At first, their relationship had been based on the fact that Rachel had felt sorry for Olivia. Poor little rich girl, Rachel had often thought of her. However, Rachel's kindness and compassion had soon grown into genuine concern, and the two young women had become true friends.

Despite their closeness, though, there were so many times Rachel could recall feeling irritated with Olivia. Frustrated beyond belief. And one of those frustrations came in the form of Olivia's unwillingness to reach her full potential, her refusal to take advantage of all the wonderful opportunities her wealthy family could provide.

With limited finances, Rachel had had to satisfy herself with attending the local community college. She'd longed to attend a major university, to encounter the vast experiences and diversity a big school could offer. And there was Olivia, whose father could have afforded to send her to any university, no matter how expensive, but who had been quite happy frittering away her education by skipping classes at the same small college where Rachel had studied hard and thrived.

And then there had been the lies and manipulations. Rachel had argued with Olivia time and time again about the inconsequential lies her friend insisted on spinning for friends and family, all in the name of controlling their emotions. It seemed important to Olivia to be seen as the underdog. She wanted people to like her—she wanted people to *do* for her—and she'd tell them anything to get what she wanted.

Having grown up in a cold, materialistic environment was the key to this flaw in Olivia's character, Rachel had decided long ago. Olivia longed for people to love her. And she'd say whatever was necessary to get the love she needed to fill the void inside her heart.

Rachel had been proud and quite pleased that the relationship she shared with Olivia was more important to her best friend than Olivia's need to control. Rachel had been clear about her feelings from the very first. She'd told Olivia, simply and honestly, that they were friends...that there was no need for game-playing between them. And Rachel had thought there hadn't been.

Until Olivia and Sloan's wedding day.

At the wedding reception, Rachel had discovered that Olivia *had* lied to her. About some very important issues.

She'd felt hurt at the time. And empty. But she'd gotten over it because she'd loved Olivia. And she'd thought Sloan had, too. If Sloan was happy to be married to Olivia, then Rachel decided she'd be happy for the both of them. As Olivia had argued all those years ago, it really hadn't mattered how they came to be together. What mattered was that they *were* together.

Rachel had thought she'd known the full truth. But what she'd discovered today was that her knowledge of the past was like an unfinished jigsaw puzzle. And Sloan had offered her the final piece that completed the picture.

The image wasn't pretty. Due to Olivia's manipulations, Sloan had spent years being the husband of a woman he'd never loved.

Since her talk with Sloan in the coffee shop, Rachel had felt an odd hollowness. All day long at the school, she'd had the feeling that something inside her was expiring. Like a fire that was slowly dying. And it wasn't until this moment that she realized what it was. Her love for Olivia was fading. Fading into a gray nothingness.

She hated to think it was happening. But there was no getting around it.

Facts were facts. And these harsh facts changed everything. Olivia had been a manipulative person. And no matter what excuses Rachel had tried to find for Olivia, the woman hadn't deserved Rachel's friendship. She hadn't deserved a man like Sloan. Or the wonderful family she'd been given.

To think of all the guilt Rachel had suffered over her own wants and desires. To think of the emotions she'd stifled. To think of the hopes and dreams she'd subdued. For years! All because she'd given her devotion, her trust, her misplaced friendship to…well, to someone who hadn't cared about anyone but herself.

Rachel's stomach gripped painfully when she thought of the secret she'd kept from Sloan for so long, all for Olivia's sake. And now that she knew the whole ugly truth about her so-called friend's loveless marriage—and the awesome guilt Sloan was, even still, carrying inside him—Rachel had to decide what she was going to do about it.

Chapter Seven

"**Y**ou're going to do just fine." Sloan took Greg's wife's hand in his, patting it reassuringly. Jane's eyes were bright with excitement as she lay on the gurney in the hospital's outpatient surgery center, not a single iota of anxiety marring her brow.

"You're going to do fine," Greg parroted.

It was plain to see that it was Greg, and not his wife, who needed comforting now that Jane was just about to undergo laser surgery. But Sloan went through the motions of crooning to the patient, for his partner's sake. He'd work on assuaging Greg's fears once Jane was in the operating room.

Jane had called Sloan last night and asked him if he could be available, not to support *her,* but to support her husband, during her surgery. Sloan had chuckled understandingly and promised Jane he'd be there to hold Greg's hand. Sloan was finding that, even though the two of them had been married only a short time, Jane knew her husband well. Anxiety fairly snapped and sparked from Greg as he stood by his wife's side.

Just then Jane's gynecologist approached, greeted them all in an upbeat and positive manner, and ushered Jane off into the operating room.

Greg's clouded gaze followed them. "You really think she'll be okay?"

"Of course." Sloan draped his arm around his friend's shoulder, gently spinning him around. "Let's go have a cup of coffee in the cafeteria while we wait. Before you know it, they'll be calling you to sit with her until she's alert enough to be taken home."

The man allowed himself to be led away from the O.R. corridor. "You're right." His quiet tone was preoccupied, spoken almost to himself. "She'll be fine."

Sloan suppressed a smile. Doctors were towers of strength for their patients. Being so was part of the job. Nearly every day of the week, he watched Greg bolster the people who sought him out for medical help. But when a member of a physician's family became ill, had an accident or needed surgery, the tower of strength quickly crumbled on its foundations. It was the emotional connection that detached a doctor from his or her normal professional objectivity.

Times like this called for friends who were willing to lend support. And Sloan was happy to do whatever he could to shore Greg up in this trying moment. Heaven knew, Greg—and Travis, too, for that matter—had certainly been there for Sloan when Olivia had been so ill.

"Not only will she be fine," Sloan said, "but once she heals, you two can look forward to getting yourselves pregnant."

This comment caused Greg to grin. He rubbed his abdomen. "Don't think I'll look too attractive being big as a barn."

"You might not," Sloan agreed. "But Jane will glow. And if you make that barn comment in front of her, just make sure you're ready to fend off the smack she's going to give you."

Greg laughed, nodding acceptance of the advice. Then his gaze grew serious. "I don't have to tell you how important this is to Jane."

Shaking his head, Sloan said, "No, you don't."

"We've tried not to get our hopes up, but..."

"I saw the test results," Sloan said. "There's no reason in the world to think this isn't going to work."

"I know. But still...it's scary. I don't want Jane to be disappointed."

They stepped into the elevator and punched the button that would take them to the first floor.

Sloan reminded him, "You've suggested this procedure to some of your patients. Any of them have complications?"

He knew the answer before he'd asked, but the question was merely meant to further ease his friend's anxiety.

Greg shook his head. "None. They all came through with flying colors."

Nodding, Sloan exited the elevator when the doors

slid open smoothly. "And the doctor you've chosen is the best. You have nothing to worry about."

But Sloan knew in his heart that the worry hazing Greg's eyes wouldn't lift until he saw Jane, conscious and coherent, after the operation. Now that he'd done all he could to encourage him, Sloan knew it was time to take Greg's mind off his wife.

As the men sat down at the table in the cafeteria with coffee and Danishes, Sloan said, "So what do you think about Travis's idea that Diana join the practice?"

Greg's expression sharpened with the change of subject.

"With her background and education, she's got plenty of experience to do the job," he told Sloan.

"I think her idea of coming in as a counselor is a great idea," Sloan said. "I think she'd be a great asset to us. And to our patients."

"Me, too." Greg added cream to his coffee. "It'll be a job, filing all that paperwork with the state to transfer her license."

"Yes, but she'll get it done."

Nodding in agreement, Greg bit into the cinnamon-and-nut-swirled pastry.

The conversation lagged while they chewed in silence.

Then, Greg said, "Speaking of office matters, what's going on between you and Rachel?"

The coffee cup in Sloan's hand nearly clattered to the table, but he held fast. The question surprised him…made him feel self-conscious, actually.

"Going on? Nothing's going on."

"Yeah, right." His friend rolled his eyes. "The

tension in the office has been as thick as shaving cream since the new year began.''

Suddenly, Sloan lost his appetite. He set down his cup, and with as much indifference as he could muster, he said, "I haven't noticed any tension."

Greg laughed loud enough to make heads turn.

"You're not a good liar, pal," he said. "The two of you have been acting like identical poles on a magnet. I've never seen people repel each other like the two of you."

"You're crazy."

But Sloan knew Greg was correct in his analogy. Since last weekend, Rachel and he had been acting like oil and water. If she was at one end of the office, he was at the other. He hated to think the people he worked with realized that something was happening between Rachel and himself.

He'd like to talk to Greg about this, but the awkwardness of the whole situation kept him silent. Rachel had been in their employ for years. Ever since they had started the practice. She'd become Greg's and Jane's friend, as well as Travis's and Diana's. Sloan felt odd about discussing her, or his feelings for her.

When Greg and Travis had first met the women in their lives, they had both called emergency meetings to discuss their troubles. However, Sloan just didn't feel right doing that. Jane and Diana had both been strangers to Sloan when those discussions had taken place. He'd felt comfortable doling out advice that was partial to his friends. But Rachel was no stranger to Greg and Travis. The men might feel ill at ease talking about her.

Besides all of that, if this conversation with Greg went any further, Sloan was sure the subject of Olivia was bound to pop up. And he simply wasn't ready to reveal to Greg all the black and ugly feelings he'd been suffering. Discussing his guilt with Rachel had been one thing. She'd been his wife's best friend, had cared about Olivia just as much as he had. And there had been more love in Rachel's heart for Olivia than there ever was in Sloan's, that was for sure. He winced at the magnitude of the guilt eddying in his gut. He turned away from the muddy river of emotions inside him. He didn't want to revisit that dark place. Not now. In fact, discussing his feelings with Rachel had probably been a mistake. Revealing his feelings—or rather, lack of them—made him look and feel like a total jerk. He wanted nothing more than to forget them. All of them.

But his conscience refused to allow that.

"Crazy or not," Greg continued after he'd swallowed, "I just have one comment to make."

Sloan found himself holding his breath.

His friend's head cocked slightly to one side and he gave a quick wink. "It's about time you noticed, ol' buddy."

Confusion etched deeply into Sloan's brow. Noticed what? he wondered.

Was Greg telling him that it was high time he found a woman? That he'd been a widower long enough? That he should shed his cloak of anguish and release his male instincts from the dark cave in which he'd imprisoned them?

Although he suspected his friend was suggesting all of those things, Sloan couldn't help but think

Greg's comment held another meaning, one that was deeper, more intimate. One that specifically involved Rachel. Taking a sip of his coffee, Sloan pondered all the possible implications.

"Tell me something, Rachel…"

Looking up from the rack of CDs she'd been searching through, Rachel saw that Sloan's dark eyes were fixed, not on her, but on the images of the young rock stars gracing the fronts of the many compact discs displayed in front of him.

"Sure," she said, her hand pausing, the heel of her palm resting on the edge of the metal stand. "I'll tell you whatever you want to know."

Their relationship, personal and professional, had become too awkward for words. The talk they'd shared this past weekend at the coffee shop *should* have helped them to grow closer. But Rachel felt so bad about the guilt Sloan harbored—not to mention the secret she'd been keeping for years—and it seemed Sloan felt self-conscious about having confided in her. They avoided each other like the black plague.

However, for all the avoiding, she was more aware of him than ever before.

The whole office had been abuzz all week long. One of the nurses, evidently unable to stand the suspense and the silence, had actually approached Rachel and asked her if she and Sloan had had some sort of disagreement. Rachel had successfully parried the woman's curiosity, but the incident made her realize that something had to be done. The wall of silence between herself and Sloan had to be broken down.

The very next time Sloan had passed her desk, Rachel had forced herself to speak to him...knowing full well that the eyes and ears of everyone they worked with were captivated by their every word and deed. She'd casually asked him what he planned to buy the girls for their birthday. Sloan had admitted he was thoroughly stumped as to what his daughters might like, and then—astoundingly—he'd asked her to go shopping with him.

With only minimal stammering, she'd agreed. And here they were, perusing CDs at one of Philadelphia's largest music stores.

"How come you..."

His hesitation seemed to hum in the air around them as his fingers stopped flipping through the plastic cases. Still, he refused to look at her.

"...disapproved of my being with Olivia?"

His question shocked her. "Disapproved? What makes you think I disapproved?"

"Oh, come on now," he said.

He pulled out a CD and glanced at the back. But something told Rachel he wasn't comprehending a word of the information printed there.

"You and Olivia shared an apartment while you went to college together," he continued. "You were there from the very beginning of my relationship with her. After only meeting me a few times, you seemed to make yourself scarce. You were never around when I came to visit."

"B-but—" thoughts tumbled, one over another, as

she tried to find her tongue ''—w-well, my absence had nothing to do with disapproval.''

There was no way she could tell him the truth. That she'd found him attractive all those years ago. That she felt drawn to his intelligence. His dark good looks. However, he was dating Olivia. And her best friend had fallen for Sloan—would have ''died without him,'' Olivia had said—so Rachel had done the only thing she could. She'd avoided Sloan as much as possible.

She felt terrible to discover he believed she had disapproved of him.

''Admit it,'' he said. ''You didn't like me.''

''I won't admit to something that's not true.'' She was upset now. How could he think such a thing? Especially when reality was just the opposite of what he believed. But there was no way she was telling him that.

''In fact,'' he pushed further, ''you disliked me so much, that when Olivia started talking marriage, you moved out of the apartment you shared with her.''

She gasped. ''I didn't leave because of *you*.'' She felt hot. Flustered. But he had been part of the reason behind her leaving. Not because she had anything against him, but because she'd been horrified by Olivia's manipulative plans for Sloan. If she hadn't left, she'd have confronted him. Told him everything. The only reason she hadn't was because she'd been under the mistaken impression that he loved Olivia.

Now, years later, she wished she had gone to him with the truth.

''It was Olivia,'' she continued. ''We had an argument. She was going to—'' Rachel stopped short, pressing her lips tightly together. "We quarreled over something that...well, over something that we simply didn't agree on."

He turned his head to look at her, and Rachel found herself run straight through by his piercing gaze.

"What was it you argued over?"

How could she tell him the truth? Olivia was the woman who had given birth to his children. If Rachel disclosed her lying ways, his thinking regarding his dead wife would surely change. He just might end up hating Olivia. The mother of his daughters.

Finally, she whispered, "It was nothing, Sloan. Nothing."

She hated lying to him. Her deceitfulness too closely resembled Olivia's behavior.

But this was different, a voice in her mind silently railed. She wasn't trying to manipulate Sloan. She wasn't attempting to control him in any way. Besides, she wasn't really lying, was she? She was simply refusing to reveal a piece of information that would surely hurt him.

Turning back toward the display of compact discs, Rachel began flipping through them. But she was so troubled by the conversation that she didn't see a single title that flashed by her frantically searching fingers.

"Here!" She jerked a plastic case from the rack. "Sasha loves Latino rock." Shoving the CD into his hands, she said, "I'm going over there to check out what's on the clearance shelf. You don't have anything against saving some money, do you?"

Without waiting for his reply, she turned on her heel and marched away.

"These will be perfect."

Sloan watched as three sweaters landed on the checkout counter. Absently reaching out, he fingered the cotton fabric of the one on top of the pile.

"You're sure?" he asked her. "They're all so different."

Rachel smiled. It was the first one he'd seen steal across her mouth since they'd made the CD purchases in the music store over an hour ago.

"Those girls may look exactly alike," Rachel said, "but they're as different as night and day and…and…well, they're all completely different. Their taste in clothing is miles apart."

He looked at the sweaters. "How will I know who gets what?"

"You're kidding me, right? Sasha loves to be noticed, so this color-block one is for her. The purple and yellow really stand out. And Sydney's favorite color is red. She'll love that one."

"I didn't know Sophie liked pink," he commented.

"Well…"

The way Rachel drew out the small word told Sloan there was more to the choice than he realized.

"I'm not sure she really likes pink," Rachel admitted. "But she's been talking about getting something pink." She shrugged. "Apparently, her new boyfriend said he thought she'd look nice in the color."

Sloan's brows rose. "We're buying a pink sweater because that little Bobby boy says we should?"

Her smile admitted the whole truth when it went lopsided and she shrugged again. And Sloan didn't think Rachel had ever looked more sexy than she did right now.

"You know—" his tone grew quiet and serious "—I'm awfully sorry things have grown so... awkward between us."

Immediately, her gaze shot toward the floor.

Gently, he touched his fingers to her chin and forced her to look him in the eye. "I mean it, Rachel. I'm sorry. I should never have unloaded on you in the coffee shop. I should never have burdened you with my—"

"Please don't ever think that I'm burdened," she rushed to interrupt, "when you talk to me about your problems. No matter what the problem. Whether it's the girls, or patients, or...or anything. I don't mind offering you a shoulder to lean on."

This kind of generosity was typical of her, and it warmed his heart.

"Listen," he told her, "we've bought the girls clothes and music and books. That certainly should be enough. What do you say about having a little fun? Just the two of us. Let's forget everything. The girls, their birthday..."

As well as the fact that I troubled you with the truth about my marriage, his brain shouted in the hesitation. The sales clerk returned with his credit card and bagged the purchases.

"...everything," he continued, "and lose ourselves in a little mindless entertainment."

"Mindless entertainment?"

The skepticism in her tone made him tip back his head and laugh. When next he looked into her lovely face, her eyes were shining with anticipation.

"I'm game," she said.

"Then you've got just the right attitude for what I have in mind."

The arcade was noisy and filled with children. Young ones with their parents and older ones on their own. Rachel couldn't see anyone older than, say, twenty, who didn't have children with them. This was definitely a place geared toward kids. But Sloan didn't seem a bit out of his element.

The two of them seized an air-hockey table, and before too long, Rachel was so overtaken by the spirit of heated competition that she no longer noticed they were the only adults who were playing games in the establishment. She'd beat him, darn it, if it was the last thing she did.

With a well-aimed shot, her puck slipped into the goal.

"I win!" She jumped up and down while punching her fists into the air.

"All right, all right," Sloan muttered. "Haven't you ever heard of good sportsmanship?"

Rachel's gasp was mingled with laughter. "You're rotten! You got to do the winner's-jump-and-shout at least six times. Quit being such a poor loser."

"Okay," he admitted. "But I did let you win that one."

Now her chin dropped, her eyes widening in disbelief. "You did not!"

Sloan was laughing, his dark eyes glittering with mischief. "It's just too easy to rile you."

She tossed him a look of teasing censure. Pointing toward the puck, she said, "One more game."

"No, no, no." He came around the table. "It's clear you've mastered this game. It's time to move on to something else. Besides, there are other people waiting to play. You don't want to deprive the children, do you?"

"You're just afraid I'll beat you again."

A grin sauntered across his mouth. "Well, there is that."

Moving to the skee-ball machines, Rachel found it nearly impossible to maneuver the palm-size wooden ball up the alley in just the right place to launch it into the high-scoring holes. Sloan, of course, seemed to score forty or fifty points with each toss. The bell-clanging alarm erupted when Sloan scored a difficult one-hundred-pointer with a well-placed shot.

Finally, the frustration became more than she could handle. "What am I doing wrong?"

After cocking a dark eyebrow at her scoreboard, he commented, "Your scoring is pretty consistent. Ten points for each ball you've tossed."

She actually growled at him. "It's impossible to score anything *lower* than ten points for each try." She knew he'd already realized this fact and that his remark was only meant to tease her further, so she socked him playfully on the arm.

"Ouch!" His wincing and rubbing was melodramatic. "You'd better cut it out or I'm going to call security."

"What you're going to do—" she pointed her finger at him, nearly coming into contact with his nose "—is show me how to score big points on this stupid game."

"Okay, okay." He laughed. "Jeez, I never knew you could be so...well, so *forceful*."

She laughed. "I have to be. How do you think I'm able to keep all your employees in line? Not to mention your daughters."

The humor they shared was warm and intoxicating.

Looking up toward the top of the machine, where the scoring holes were located, Sloan said, "Maybe you're throwing the ball too hard. Aiming for the highest-scoring holes. That'll throw everything off. Shoot for the lower-scoring holes in the middle of the scoreboard. It isn't always wise to go for the highest prize."

But the highest prize is the only one worth having. The phrase soughed across her mind like a delicate summer breeze.

The thought brought to life every nerve ending in her body, and awareness trilled across every inch of her skin. Sloan moved in close behind her so that his chest was up against her back. The heated scent of him swirled around her like a protective blanket and she wanted to sink into it, revel in it.

He reached around her, bending to retrieve a wooden ball from its bin, and when he did so, some part of his body brushed against her bottom. A delicious shiver coursed up her backbone, making the delicate hairs on her neck stand on end. She inhaled a ragged breath at the sudden tension in the air.

"Let's see if I can improve your technique."

His whisper was delectable against her ear, and the urge to close her eyes, to savor the sound of him, the nearness of him, the smell of him, became more than she could bear. Inadvertently, she wet her lips, waiting breathlessly for his next move, his next word.

Ever so gently, he placed the skee ball into her hand, the wood hard and cool against her skin. Sightless, her sense of the physical world seemed to become keener, more sensitive. His big palm slid to securely cradle her hand, his strong fingers warm against hers. When he drew back their hands, she instinctively bent her knees, his shoulder against the back of hers, their bodies flowing in perfect synchronicity.

In the periphery of her consciousness, she heard the ball rolling up the alley, wood against wood.

"Ah, Rachel."

It sounded like a tragic moan, and she twisted her head, languidly lifting her eyelids to find him staring down into her face. The air tightened, and time seemed to become sluggish as the seconds thudded, thudded along, pulsing like a lazy heartbeat.

Their gazes seemed to play on some imaginary playground. Sensuous games. Erotic games. His fingers drew slow, tiny circles on the back of her hand. Then he reached up and gingerly captured her jaw in the U between his index finger and thumb.

His chocolate-brown eyes seemed to melt, growing even darker with what Rachel perceived to be overwhelming passion. Her knees felt as if they'd turned to warm plastic, malleable and weak, and she was afraid she just might slide right underneath the ancient arcade machine.

"What is going on between us?"

She didn't answer his question. *Couldn't* answer his question. All she could do was fill her lungs, slowly, fully, with air. It was either that or lose consciousness altogether.

"Every time we're alone," he whispered, "I feel this overpowering need to…to—"

"Dr. Radcliff!"

Chapter Eight

His hand dropped from her face and he stepped away from her. Amazingly, even with a mere six inches of space between them, Rachel felt suddenly chilled to the bone. And the buzzing and clanging going on around her actually hurt her ears. How had she become so deaf to the loud noises in the crowded, bustling arcade?

She turned her attention to the boy who had called out to Sloan, her eyes widening a fraction when she recognized him. He was Sophie's friend, young Bobby Snyders.

"Is Sophie with you?" Bobby asked Sloan, adding a quick, "Sir."

"No, she isn't."

Bobby looked baffled. "Sydney or Sasha?"

Sloan simply shook his head in silent answer.

"Oh."

Why, the child's almost comical expression

seemed to ask, was Sophie's father hanging out in the mall arcade without his daughters? Evidently, he'd deemed the game room to be strictly a kids' domain.

"Well—" the boy looked around him, awkwardness and unspoken curiosity creeping into his face in the form of cheek-flushing embarrassment "—tell Sophie...that, ah...that I'll call her. Please." The final word was added in as rushed afterthought, just as the "sir" had been a moment before.

Rachel thought Bobby's mother would be proud to know the manners she'd most probably drilled into him had left an indelible mark.

"I'll do that," Sloan said.

The boy offered a half smile. "I'm looking forward to the party."

"Yeah, well, don't buy Sophie anything pink," Sloan told him. "I've already taken care of that."

Bobby sauntered away from them after a departing nod. It was clear from his expression that he found adults to be odd creatures deserving a wide berth.

Sloan turned his dark eyes on her, and Rachel felt that the romantic moment had well and truly passed. The magical spell had been broken. All that remained was that ungainly awkwardness that always had them both shifting their bodies and averting their gazes from each other.

Instinctively knowing it was time to go home, the two of them silently gathered up their packages and headed for the door.

Less than thirty minutes later, Sloan pulled his car into the parking lot of Rachel's apartment complex.

"No need for you to park," she told him. "The super installed a new security door. No one can get in without a key. I'll be perfectly safe on my own."

"You're sure?"

"Sure, I'm sure." She forced a smile onto her lips, but his expression remained fixed.

Strangely, the moment swelled, throbbed. The sudden tears that gathered in her eyes startled her. She was thankful for the darkness. Despite her best efforts, the corners of her mouth drooped, and her heart sank in her chest. What was behind this sudden welling of emotion?

Her relationship with Sloan was taking on the characteristics of an out-of-control roller-coaster ride. Up one minute and down the next, and hairpin curves and heart-stopping loops that were enough to make even the strongest of people feel battered, bruised and broken.

Rachel only wished those high, euphoric moments lasted a little longer. Like the one in the arcade this evening, or the one in his kitchen when they baked all those cookies together, or the one on the dance floor on New Year's Eve. The summits sure seemed short-lived compared to the deep valleys, which seemed to meander on forever.

The need to escape made Rachel reach hastily for the door latch.

"Wait."

She shifted around to face him.

"Don't go just yet," he said.

Her body went tense all over.

"Don't you think we should talk? Don't you think

we should…well, that we should address what's been happening between us?''

Like the wings of a frightened hummingbird, her heart fluttered. She swallowed. Moistened her lips. But words refused to come into her brain or onto her tongue.

He slid the gearshift into park, and then twisted his body so that he was facing her more fully.

"I mean," he continued, "at first I thought it was all me. I felt terrible about kissing you on New Year's Eve." He lifted his hand, palm up. "Not that I didn't want to. I did. What I felt bad about was that I'd thought I'd somehow taken advantage of you… that I'd—"

"I understand," she croaked. Her voice sounded as rusty as a weathered tin can.

"But then when we were baking together…and things between us…well, when things heated up…"

How could he chuckle at a time like this? she wondered. How could he find anything in this situation humorous?

"You flirted with me that night," he said. "Or, rather, I thought that you did. And then this evening in the arcade…you wanted me to kiss you. At least, I felt that you did."

She found his uncertainty so darned charming.

Sloan's head tilted to one side, his dark gaze growing serious. "If I'm wrong here, I need to know. I need you to tell me—"

"You're not wrong."

The breath he exhaled could only have been described as relieved.

Seconds passed, and finally the silence in the cab of the car seemed to pulse.

"So," he said at last, "what is this? What's happening between the two of us?"

It was fear that kept her from revealing to him what was—and had been—happening to her. She'd lived so long with the love she'd felt for him, with the silence of it, the hiding of it, that she simply couldn't imagine what her life would be like if the truth were known. Her whole existence would be forever changed.

"This…this attraction we're feeling is pretty strong."

Her focus zeroed in on his mouth. On the movement of his lips and how shockingly sensual she found it. The fact that he was actually commenting on their personal relationship—not their working together at the office, or her connection with his girls—but their own intimate association, was utterly mindblowing.

Through the hazy chaos of her thoughts, she found herself nodding her agreement with the opinion he'd just voiced.

"Maybe—" his tone got softer, his fingers toying with the end of one curling tress of her hair "—we should allow ourselves to…well, to acknowledge what's going on between us. And t-to…well, to explore it."

He swallowed, and then his tongue slid out to moisten his silken lips. The pole lamps in the parking lot, high overhead, threw shadows across the sharp angles of his face. But even in the dim light, Rachel could see his nervousness, his uncertainty, hear the tension in his voice.

The emotions coursing through her were so odd. She should be dancing with joy. Having Sloan notice her should be a dream come true. Having him actually admit to wanting her...that seemed to her like some unreachable fantasy—a fantasy that should have her feeling utterly blissful.

So why was her whole body trembling with trepidation?

Wasn't there a saying that those things that seemed too good to be true, usually were?

Too good to be true. That's exactly how she saw this.

"You're awfully quiet."

His words sounded stentorian after the silence, raw and gorged and waiting.

"I—I'm just scared, is all."

A tiny smile had his mouth cocking up at one corner.

"Boy, oh, boy—" his dark head shook back and forth "—I can relate to what you're feeling."

"You can?"

He nodded. "I sure can."

The touch of his fingers against her jaw was gentle, but Rachel found it jolting. Powerful.

"We have a lot of talking to do, you and I," he said. Then he murmured an aside, "As well as a lot of thinking."

Her head bobbed in agreement. She was about to invite him in, but he said, "However, I promised the girls I'd be home in time to read over their science reports. They had to write a detailed account of a scientist who had contributed something significant to humanity in the past hundred years.''

"Right," she said. Disappointment and relief surged through her at the same time, leaving her with a feeling that was indescribable. Like pipes flooded with hot water and cold oil. The substances couldn't blend, so they resulted in a swirling, churning, freezing, burning confusion to the senses.

"But…if you don't mind…''

There it was again in his tone, she thought, that uncertainty that she found so darned appealing. The doubt he was clearly experiencing shuttered his expression, glittered in his dark gaze, made his whole body tense.

"Would it be okay if I kissed you good-night?''

Trepidation billowed in her chest like a volcanic cloud, dark and threatening. But how could she say anything but yes? This was what she wanted, wasn't it? This was what she'd hoped for.

She nodded, and he took her in his arms. The warmth of him was delectable. The scent of him, mouthwateringly delicious. The solid mass of him, safe and secure.

His mouth slanted down over hers, and Rachel felt as if she were being attacked by his need—an attack she didn't mind surrendering to. Parting her lips, she bid him enter, and it was an invitation he didn't hesitate to accept.

Passion vibrated through her, through them both. Rachel could feel the heat of it in the close confines of the car. Soon, her breath was coming in short pants. His was, too. And if they hadn't been in the parking lot in Sloan's car…if they'd been someplace private, like her apartment…if the girls hadn't been waiting…who knew where this encounter might have ended?

His hand slid down over her shoulder, eased between the facings of her wool coat and cupped the fullness of her breast. If his lips hadn't been clamped over hers, she'd have gasped at the utter pleasure of his touch. He kneaded gently, his thumb rubbing the nub of her nipple until it budded to life under the fabric of her blouse. Every inch of her flesh became supersensitive. Her clothing felt cumbersome and restrictive. She wanted nothing more than to feel his fingertips on her bare skin, feel his kiss on the most secret places of her body.

Her head lolled against the seat back as she dragged breath into her lungs, and immediately, Sloan's hot, moist mouth found her neck. Luscious shivers coursed throughout her body. Her eyes rolled closed, desire building, building inside her. Bubbling. Simmering. Hot. Breathtaking.

Somehow, in what seemed like the speed of light, he'd managed to unfasten the buttons of her blouse. His fingertips scorched the tender flesh of her abdomen, the valley between her breasts, as he worked to unhook the front clasp of her bra.

He paused, and her every instinct silently shouted for her to help him. Dragging her hands from where they had been smoothing over the taut muscles of his neck, combing through his thick hair, she reached toward her bra. But his quelling hands on hers forced her eyes to open, even though being roused from this fuzzy, sensual state was the last thing she wanted. The frantic need pulsing thickly through her blood had her searching his face, her silent plea practically begging him to continue his onslaught of touching, kissing.

This encounter surpassed her wildest imaginings, her most intoxicating dreams.

She noticed that he wasn't looking at her, but over her shoulder to somewhere outside the car.

"What is it?" She felt suddenly alarmed. "Is someone there?"

"No," he quickly assured her. "We're quite alone. But…"

"But what?"

Then his gaze did find hers, and his eyes were clouded with some unnamable emotion. Something dark. Unpleasant.

"It's nothing."

His tone was husky, barely audible.

"Of course it's something." She sat up straighter, unwittingly reaching to close the front of her blouse. "What?"

"Over these last few weeks," he began, "I've found that being with you makes me happy. Very happy."

After a moment, she stammered, "W-well, isn't that a good thing?"

"It should be," he admitted. Quietly, he repeated, "It should be."

Something in his tone mortified Rachel, made her feel humiliated. And with shaking fingers, she worked to button her blouse, straighten her clothing, smooth her mussed hair. Sloan was lost somewhere in his thoughts. So much so that he didn't even realize what she was doing. Or why.

"I don't think I can do this," he told her. "I wronged her. Terribly. I don't deserve to be happy."

There was no need for him to put a name to the *her* he'd mentioned. Rachel knew who he meant. So, the wall was still between them. No, not a wall. A tombstone. A tombstone etched with the name of a dead woman.

"He really said that?" Diana asked. "That he didn't deserve to be happy?"

Rachel nodded. "And it isn't the first time he's said it, either."

"You have to tell him." Jane's eyes were wide with disbelief once Rachel had unloaded her whole sordid story.

Looking at Diana, Rachel watched as after a moment's contemplation, she nodded her head in agreement.

"But, how can I?" Rachel argued. "Olivia was the mother of Sloan's children. He was married to her for *years*. How can I reveal to Sloan that his dead wife wasn't as innocent and pure-hearted as he thought she was? I'd be tainting his memories of her. The girls ought to be able to remember their mother with love. They ought to be able to cherish their thoughts of her."

Rachel felt as if she were between a rock and a hard place with no way out. And the pressure was incredible. She simply couldn't imagine revealing Olivia's true nature. She just couldn't imagine all the awful events the truth might set in motion.

"I agree," Diana said, "with what you say about

the girls and their memory of Olivia. But you won't be telling *them* a thing.''

"Yes,'' Jane rushed to add, ''this is between you and Sloan. Just the two of you. The girls never need to know.''

Rachel looked from one woman to the other. They were right. She knew it. Still, she felt hesitant about confronting Sloan.

"I-it's just that,'' she tried to explain, words coming haltingly, ''I—I feel so strange just thinking about revealing the details about Olivia's behavior. It would be cruel. She's *dead*.''

The last word was accentuated, as if that fact alone was enough to justify her reasons for not coming clean to Sloan with all she knew.

"You're making it sound as if you'll be gossiping,'' Jane said. ''This is different. This wouldn't be spreading idle rumors. You'll be revealing cold, hard facts. And it sure wouldn't be cruel.'' She hesitated, as if she had more she wanted to say, but couldn't quite figure out her thoughts. Finally, all she was able to add was, ''It wouldn't.''

However, Rachel didn't miss the fact that, as sure as Jane was about her opinion, the woman couldn't seem to explain just why this wouldn't be a brutal act on Rachel's part.

As Rachel saw it, telling Sloan the secret about Olivia and her pregnancy would forever alter the man's thoughts and feelings where his deceased wife was concerned. Did she really want to be responsible for that?

Diana reached out and touched Rachel's forearm.

"Telling the truth about Olivia isn't going to hurt her. As you said, she's dead."

The Native American woman seemed to exude a calm that Rachel found wonderfully comforting.

"But, Rachel, you know in your heart that only the honest truth will truly heal those who were left behind."

"So we're in agreement?" Travis narrowed his eyes across the conference table at Greg.

Greg nodded. "We do everything we can to get him to spill his guts."

"The man needs to talk," Travis said. "He's been holding everything in too long."

The two men were waiting for Sloan so they could have their morning conference.

"You know that, and I know that," Greg muttered, "but our good buddy doesn't think he needs to lean on his friends."

"We leaned on him when we had our women problems."

"We did, indeed." Greg grinned. "But the problems all got ironed out, didn't they?"

"They sure did." Travis's mouth quirked up at the corners, too. Then, he sobered. "You sure you don't mind being the one who brings up the topic?"

"I don't mind. How hard could it be? We need to help him out. This kind of stuff is what friends are for."

Travis said, "We have to be smooth about it, though. We'll talk about our own love interests first, then we'll ease into—"

"Trust me, won't you?"

Just then Sloan entered the conference room having heard Greg's whiny tone. "Travis, if I were you I wouldn't trust the man farther than I could throw him."

"Which wouldn't be far, you wimp," Greg jeered good-naturedly.

Travis's gaze glittered with mischief. "You *are* the old man of the group."

"And I'd be happy to take either one of you on," Sloan shot back. "Just not in the office. That would be most unprofessional."

Greg murmured, "Convenient excuse, if you ask me."

Travis only snickered.

As Sloan sat down he was shaking his head, placing two patient files in front of him on the table. "So, what schemes are you two hatching in here this morning?"

"Schemes?" Greg's spine straightened. "What makes you think we were scheming?"

Holding up a palm in surrender, Sloan said, "Hey, I was joking."

"Of course, he was." Travis narrowed his eyes at Greg.

Sloan couldn't help but come to the conclusion that his friends were acting mighty suspicious this morning. But he simply didn't have the mental energy it would take to try to figure out their behavior.

He'd spent the last two days worrying over his problem with Rachel. He wanted her. Man, oh, man, how he wanted her. But those monstrous dark clouds descended on him each and every time he attempted to act on his feelings.

Greg lifted his mug of coffee. "Let's have a toast. To me and Jane."

"Hey!" Travis reached for his drink. "The operation was a success?"

"It sure was," Greg announced. "Soon we can start trying for a baby."

Sloan wasn't in much of a celebratory mood since his personal life was in such a shambles, but how could he not feel happy for Greg and Jane?

"That's wonderful!" he said, lifting his own coffee mug high.

"Let's hear it for the fun part of becoming a parent." Greg grinned.

"To the fun part," Travis parroted, tipping up his mug.

Sloan added, "And may all that fun yield results."

After they had a moment to settle, Travis said, "Diana's filed the first round of forms to the state medical board."

"Great!" Greg said.

"I say we get her in here practicing as soon as possible," Sloan commented. Then he asked Travis, "How are the wedding plans coming?"

"They're moving along." Travis reached out and picked up the pen that was lying on the table. "Diana has it in her mind to make the ceremony a conglomeration of what we would think of as a traditional religious service and the Kolheek marriage ritual. I hope the wedding guests aren't upset."

"Why should they be?" Sloan asked. "It's your wedding. You and Diana should have whatever kind of ceremony you want. Ancient, traditional, new-age, or a mixture of everything."

"Yeah," Greg agreed. Grinning, he added, "Even if it means everyone has to strip naked and stand on their heads."

"You'd love that, wouldn't you?" Sloan said, his tone full of devilment.

"You've got that right! In fact, I'd be the first man out of his trousers."

"You'd also be the first man to incite a laughing riot," Travis said.

Sloan grinned. "Or a pity party."

"Oh." Greg shook his head. "You guys are low. Don't you know it's rude to make fun of a man's…" He paused a second as he searched for a fitting noun. Finally, he grinned and said, *"Manhood?"*

"But this is *your* manhood we're talking about," Sloan said.

"Or lack there of." The snicker Travis was trying to control bested him. "And who better to make fun of your deficiencies than your best friends?"

Greg tossed a rude expression at Travis. Then he sobered. "Enough about me and my endowments… but while we're on the subject of *matters of the heart*—"

"Is that what the subject was?" Sloan murmured, one corner of his mouth tipping upward.

"In my book…yeah," Greg responded. "Sex and romance. One and the same."

Sloan caught Travis's eye. "How does Jane live with this guy?"

"Beats me."

Then Greg leveled his gaze on Sloan. "And how's *your* love life?"

He was so taken aback by the question, Sloan's brows shot toward the ceiling. "I beg your pardon?"

"Your love life," Greg repeated. "How's it going? Everyone in the office has noticed the thing you've got going with Rachel."

Irritation flooded his face. He could feel the heat rise, higher and higher.

"I'd be happy to tell you all about it," he said, working hard to keep his voice quiet and controlled, "if I thought it was any of your business."

"Look," Greg said, seemingly unaware of Sloan's anger, "you need to talk. I tried before, but you shut me down. You've got to realize that whatever you two are going through affects the working environment around here. The atmosphere is loose and friendly one day, cold as a cadaver the next."

"Let us help you," Travis pleaded, ignoring Greg's offensive metaphor. "We all need help, now and then."

His friends had the best of intentions, Sloan knew that. And Travis was right. They had both talked about their problems with the women in their lives at some point. But Sloan didn't feel he could do that. The guilt that plagued him had him feeling the exact opposite of masculine. There was no way he could admit this weakness.

"Both of us spilled our guts when we needed advice," Greg reminded him. "What kind of friends are we if you can't come to us when you need to talk?"

"You're right," Sloan admitted. Then he tried to calm his mind so he could figure out what facts he could, and couldn't, reveal to his buddies. Finally, he said, "You're right, too, when you said that…well, that there's something between me and Rachel."

"Now we're getting somewhere." Greg rested his elbow on the edge of the table.

"She and I discussed exploring our feelings." Sloan spoke slowly, deciding on how much to disclose as he went along. "But…well, I don't think it's going to work out."

There, he thought, that should do it. That should certainly be enough to satisfy his friends' curiosity and their desire to help.

Ever-so-quietly, Travis asked, "What made you come to that conclusion so quickly?"

What, indeed? Sloan's mind became a whirlwind of thoughts. He didn't have it in him to admit the truth—that guilt tormented him to the point that he couldn't even hold the woman of his dreams, let alone kiss her or make wild and passionate love to her.

"Why would you give up," Greg wondered aloud, "when you've barely begun?"

Why would he give up? his friends wanted to know.

Well, what he wanted to know was why were they ganging up on him?

"Because…well, because…" He stumbled over the words, halting in midsentence as his brain scrambled for an explanation. "Because I revealed some facts about my past that make me look…well, that made me look bad."

"What are you talking about?" Travis's frown indicated that he didn't believe a word he was hearing. "What could you have possibly said that would make you look anything but the stellar person you are?''

"Spill it." There was nothing ceremonious about Greg's coaxing. "It can't be as bad as you think."

Sloan sighed. "I told her that I didn't love my wife when we got married. That I only married Olivia because she'd become pregnant with the girls."

The room went utterly quiet.

Finally, Greg said, "Wow, Sloan. I never knew."

More seconds ticked by as the men contemplated what they'd just learned.

"That doesn't make you look bad," Travis said. "In fact, from a woman's perspective, I think your actions make you look quite honorable."

"Stupid and gullible, too," Greg quipped with a chuckle.

When neither of the other two men laughed, Greg subdued his humorous streak. "I'm with Travis on this one," he said. "Rachel would see your behavior as admirable."

Honorable? Admirable? Sloan was sure those were the very last adjectives he'd use to describe himself and his behavior.

Suddenly the need to be alone caught Sloan up like a tornado. He stood in a quick, jerky motion, picking up the patient files. "I appreciate your wanting to help, guys. I really do. But I just can't talk about this."

He scooted the chair back, got to his feet and walked out the door. He paused in the hall, trying to shove his way out of the guilty fog that had enveloped him.

"Hey, Sloan," Greg called after him, "come back."

But he didn't go back. He couldn't.

Then Sloan heard Travis said, "Stupid? Gullible? What are you, an idiot?"

"Hey, I was making a joke."

"And what ever happened to easing into the subject?" Travis asked. "*How's your love life?* is *not* easing into it." Travis clicked his tongue in obvious disgust. "That's the *last* time I trust you to be smooth."

Chapter Nine

Sloan met Rachel as she was coming out of his office door. That damned awkward air had become worse since they'd gone shopping together. Why hadn't he tried to shop for presents for his girls on his own?

Who was he trying to delude? It hadn't been the shopping that had gotten him into trouble with Rachel. The pivotal moment had been when he'd proclaimed his desire for her, only to announce that he couldn't bring himself to act on his feelings. No wonder she didn't want to look him in the face.

"I left some forms on your desk that need signing," she told him. Then she dipped her head as if to duck around him.

"Wait, Rachel." He reached out and put his hand on her shoulder.

One of the part-time filing clerks who worked in the office looked their way and then made a valiant

but unsuccessful attempt to look as if she wasn't interested in them.

"Would you come into my office for a sec?" he
said to Rachel. "I want to ask you something."

Without a word, she turned and went back inside.
Sloan followed her and closed the door.

"I, um..." He hesitated, then started again. "I
know that I've put our relationship under a little
strain."

She remained silent, still refusing to look him in
the eye.

"But I'm hoping," he continued, "that this isn't
going to keep you from attending the girls' birthday
party this Saturday."

Her gaze met his. "Of course I'll come to the
party. I wouldn't dream of missing it."

Relief flooded through him. "Good." He pressed
his lips together, garnering the courage to ask her
advice. "Listen, I need some help. I just called the
bakery this morning. I ordered three identical cakes.
The lady on the phone suggested novelty cakes. She
told me what they had to offer, and I chose ladybugs.
I used to call the girls my little ladybugs. But...as
soon as I hung up, I started having second thoughts
about what I ordered." He felt his nose wrinkle with
the doubt that burned in his belly. "What do you
think?"

"I think," she began slowly, "that your second
thoughts just might be telling you something important. And I also think you need to listen to them."

He groaned, moving past Rachel. He skirted a
bookcase, launched himself into his chair and
grabbed the telephone book that had been shoved to

one corner of his desktop. As he flipped through its pages, looking for the bakery's telephone number, he heaved a sigh.

"Ladybugs," he muttered. "What was I thinking?" His fingers paused and he glanced up into Rachel's golden-brown eyes. "So what should I order? They offer cakes shaped like flowers. A daisy. A big black-eyed Susan. They also had one cake that looked like a poppy. And they had lots to offer sports-minded kids. A soccer ball. Basketball. Football. A football helmet, even. But none of those are really appropriate."

Why did he always feel at an absolute loss when it came to providing things for his little girls? The expression on Rachel's face told him that all of the choices he'd just listed were completely wrong.

"Ah, Rachel," he groaned, running agitated fingers through his hair. "Help me get his right. This is an important day for the girls."

For a moment, she didn't speak. And for a moment, Sloan feared that she meant to turn her back on him.

It was what he deserved, he knew. To have toyed with her affections as he had. To have danced with her so closely, so intimately. To have kissed her so thoroughly. To have spoken with such candor. To have admitted that he wanted her. Only to withdraw himself from her. He was an idiot to believe she would help him now.

His behavior toward her had been inexcusable. Over and over again.

"Sloan, I love those girls."

Her voice was filled to the brim with sincerity.

There seemed to be something else in her tone, too. Something more she wanted to say. But in the end she only glanced over his shoulder and out the window at the chilly January scene he knew was behind him.

When she did look at him again, she drew her lips back in a smile. "Sophie and Sydney and Sasha mean the world to me. I'll do everything I can to see that they're happy."

His throat knotted with emotion. Rachel was quite a woman.

"What you need to do," she continued, "is rethink the whole idea of a novelty cake."

"But—" he shook his head "—the party. Don't we need a fancy cake?"

"Sure. But we don't need one shaped like an insect, or a flower, or sports equipment."

She was fighting the urge to chuckle at him. He could plainly tell. One corner of her mouth was twitching, and he found it sexy as hell.

"The girls are going to be teens." She raised her brows as she stressed that last word. "They want to be thought of as grown-up. They want a grown-up cake."

"A grown-up cake?"

This time her humor got the best of her and laughter bubbled up from someplace deep in her throat. If her half smile had been sexy, her laugh was tremendously titillating.

Desire curled, slow and hot, in the pit of his gut. And the solidness, the sheer density of the desire he felt made his mouth go dry. The need roiling inside him, he knew, would churn up some very dark feelings if he didn't get control of it quickly.

"Yes, a grown-up cake. A simple, double-layered, rectangular-shaped cake with writing on the top and a few flowers for decoration."

That thought had never entered his head. "You really think so?"

A few tendrils had escaped the pins that held her hair in a French twist, and they swayed as she nodded emphatically. "I really think so." Then she added, "One cake with all three names on it. Believe me, that's what will make them happy. I'm sure of it."

She smiled, and his heart started to pound.

He was sure his hand was trembling as he reached up to scrub at the back of his neck. He must get a grip on his runaway libido. He refused to be controlled by testosterone.

"It'll cost less, too." Had it been his imagination, or had his voice come out sounding wobbly and tinny? He swallowed, did his best to tamp down the myriad of emotions coursing through his bloodstream, lava-hot.

"Thanks, Rachel."

"No problem. And I am looking forward to the party on Saturday."

The muscles in his cheeks felt frozen, but he forced them to draw up into a smile to match her own. "Me, too."

One second lengthened into two, then into three. He wanted desperately to reach out to her, to round the desk and take her in his arms. But dank, musty feelings of guilt were too close to the surface, and the dark emotions made him curl his fingers into a fist and lower his hand into his lap.

"If there's nothing else," she said, "I guess I should get back to work."

"I think I'm okay now," he told her. Indicating the phone book with a single nod of his head, he added, "I'll just give the bakery a call and I'll be all set."

She seemed reluctant to leave. And every moment she remained was torture for Sloan. He could tell that working with her, day in and day out, was going to quickly become more than he could bear.

At the door she paused, her hand hovering just above the knob. Her sigh made him frown. Still, she lingered.

Finally, he felt impelled to ask, "Rachel, is everything okay?"

She turned to face him, trouble clouding her honeyed gaze. Deep trouble.

"No," she said, her tone barely a whisper. "Everything *isn't* okay. In fact, *nothing* is okay. You're not. I'm not. Nothing is."

He had no idea how to respond to her sudden and very unexpected outburst. So he didn't. He just sat at his desk, knowing full well his face was awash with the bewilderment besieging him.

Again she sighed as she came toward him, lowering herself into the leather chair sitting at an angle to his desk. When her gaze rose to meet his, the distress she so obviously felt not only shadowed her eyes, it had etched itself into her beautiful face.

"You're scaring me, Rachel," he told her. "What's going on?"

She expelled a third sigh. Whatever she had to say, she was mighty reluctant to put it into words.

"I have some information," she began. Then she looked down at the carpet between her feet.

He watched her nibble on her top lip. When she tipped up her chin to look him in the face, the worry in her gaze was mingled with another emotion. Resolve.

She started again. "I have something to tell you. Something you're not going to like. Something that just m-might...something that just might change everything." Almost to herself, she whispered, "I do hope it changes everything for you."

His perplexity swelled until it actually made him feel dizzy and disoriented. What on earth could she be alluding to? What could she know that she would think would affect him in such a manner that would have her so ridden with anxiety?

He could keep silent no longer.

"Is it the girls? Have they told you something? Are they in some kind of trouble at school?"

"No, Sloan," she told him. "This has nothing to do with the girls. Well, it has everything to do with them...but it has nothing to do with them."

Impatience flared like a bolt of lightning on a stormy night. "You're talking in riddles now."

"Sloan—"

The plea he read in her eyes snuffed out the small annoyance that had flashed inside him.

"—please promise me you'll try not to get angry. Please."

The anxiety fairly pulsing off her transferred itself to him. Apprehension seized him. Shook him to the core. His spine tingled with it. The nerves just beneath his flesh prickled.

"If you don't tell me what's on your mind," he told her quietly, "I feel like I'm going to crawl right out of my skin. How can the girls have everything to do with this as well as nothing? You're not making sense."

The urge to pace was strong, and it was all he could do to remain seated.

"I'm sorry. You'll understand soon enough." She reached up and tucked an errant strand of hair behind her ear. "It has nothing to do with them because what I'm about to tell you happened before they were born."

An ominous cloud descended upon him, and he felt as if he'd swallowed a brick.

"This has something to do with Olivia." He phrased his words as a statement, but there was plenty of inquiry in his tone. Plenty of ill-omened reluctance, too, because all of a sudden he wasn't even sure he wanted to hear what she had to say.

Rachel nodded silently.

He knew time hadn't slowed; however, it felt as if each second was lumbering by, thick and stolid and unwieldy.

"Olivia was my best friend," Rachel began. "I loved her. Very much. But she wasn't an easy person to have as a friend. If fact, it was quite difficult for me at times."

Sloan nearly chuckled at the irony of what Rachel was saying. His deceased wife hadn't been an easy person for him to live with, either. And she had made his life difficult on more occasions than he could name. It was almost funny to discover that Rachel had had the same opinion of Olivia all this time and he'd never known it.

"I'm sure you know," Rachel continued, "Olivia was always determined to have her own way."

Now Sloan did laugh, softly shaking his head back and forth. "She was that."

"Usually, people like Olivia…" Rachel paused a moment as if she were pondering her words, wanting to get them just right. "Strong-willed people usually gravitate toward weak-willed people. People they can easily manipulate. But Olivia wasn't like that. She was drawn to other strong-willed people, like you and me."

"But that didn't keep her from trying to manipulate us."

Averting her gaze, Rachel pressed her lips together, expelling a deep, sad-sounding breath.

"Olivia was a complex person," she continued. "She wanted her own way. She was manipulative. But she also had a conscience."

He watched as something akin to humor sparked in Rachel's golden eyes.

"It often took a while for her conscience to kick in," she quipped. "Sometimes years. But it always did. Eventually."

There was love in her tone, in her words, in the faith she had in her best friend. There was a poignancy there, too. Sloan heard it. And he envied Rachel those feelings. They were emotions he wished he felt when thinking of Olivia. But all he was walloped with was guilt and self-blame, and, yes, he'd admit it, a hefty chunk of resentment, too.

"Rachel," he cut in, "I appreciate all the things that you're saying. But you're not telling me anything I don't already know."

"Be patient. I need to start at the beginning. Otherwise, you might be so angry with Olivia t-that... that it'll color your whole view of the past. And I don't want that to happen."

The conversation was getting more peculiar by the second.

Finally, the suspense became more than he could bear. "Rachel, what did Olivia do?"

When she refused to be rushed, he rested his elbow on the open phone book, absently pinched at his chin between the knuckle of his index finger and thumb, and waited.

"There were several times during our friendship—" her voice was quiet "—when I simply had to take a break from her. From our friendship. Olivia would try to get me to do something with her or for her, something that I didn't want to do, or she'd announce some outlandish plan to get her father to send the two of us on a holiday, or she'd reveal her intention to do something I thought was wrong." Her tone lowered an octave as she added, "Terribly wrong."

The brick in his stomach suddenly increased in density, and Sloan was certain it had grown into a cement block.

"Let me help you out," he told her. "Olivia's pregnancy. That's what we're talking about here, isn't it? There was nothing accidental about it, was there? It was planned, wasn't it?"

She winced as each question hit her.

"I suspected as much, after she told me

about…her condition," he said. "But what good would it have done to accuse her of such a thing? It would have only stirred up strife. The deed was done. All that was left was for me to take responsibility for my actions."

"She loved you. You do understand that?"

A bleakness filled his mind. His whole body. "Do you really think she understood what love is?"

"I think—" Rachel's tone brightened with hope "—that in the end she did. She really did."

He couldn't help but look away, dubious.

"She told me how much she loved you," Rachel said. "You were the one, she said. The one she wanted to spend her life with. But she was so impatient. You still had three years of college left. And then medical school. She said she simply couldn't wait that long." Her gaze slid away yet again.

"So she planned to get herself pregnant so we'd have to get married."

Rachel didn't meet his eyes; she only nodded her head in answer.

Finally, she did look at him. "But she never expected you to drop out of school. She thought she had it all figured out. Her father would step in. He'd pay for your college tuition while all of you—you, she and the baby—would live with her parents."

"Well, like you said," Sloan replied, "she was drawn to strong-willed people. I couldn't see myself being kept by Olivia's father. A man would have to be completely worthless, a freeloading bum, not to be humiliated by the mere idea of being kept like that."

Her tone was a breathy whisper as she said, "Yes."

He was glad she understood his reason for quitting school, for not allowing Olivia's father to pay his way through college...through life. He wouldn't have been able to live with himself.

"Anyway," Rachel said, "when Olivia told me her plan, I was furious with her. I ranted and raved. Told her how wrong it was. Finally, I threatened to tell you. And that's when she changed her mind. She said she wouldn't—that she couldn't really go through with it. I was relieved. But I was so disillusioned that she'd devised such a scheme that I needed to put some space between us." She sighed. "And that's—"

Her voice caught and she stopped. Then, looking down at her lap where her fingers were tightly entwined, she said, "And that's why I wasn't around much."

"So you weren't really avoiding me," he said, "because you disapproved of me."

Her gaze remained downcast. "I disapproved of Olivia. I didn't like the fact that my best friend could be such a schemer. I just needed to distance myself from the friendship."

Sloan got the distinct impression that she was holding something back. But he didn't press her. Instead, he said, "Okay, so you've revealed that Olivia planned to get pregnant. It's not really surprising news, Rachel, since, as I told you, I suspected it from the beginning. You don't need to feel as if you've sentenced me to life in prison or something."

"But I haven't told you the worst of it."

His brows rose. There was more to the story?

"I'd moved out of the apartment we had shared."

Sloan nodded. "I remember."

"I'd stopped calling Olivia. Stopped visiting her."

He only stared, feeling itchy with anxiety over what might be coming.

"When the wedding invitation arrived in the mail," she said, "I went right away to see her. I confronted her straight out. I asked her if she'd trapped you." Rachel closed her eyes. "She was so smooth. So suave. And so happy. She convinced me that there hadn't been any need to trick you. She wasn't pregnant. You wanted to marry her. Couldn't wait to do so, in fact. The two of you were in love." Her gaze imparted utter misery. "Sloan, Olivia wasn't pregnant when the two of you married."

"But...she told me she was. I wouldn't have married her otherwise."

"I knew she wasn't pregnant," she continued as if she hadn't heard his protest. "But I wasn't aware that you didn't know it. And I didn't discover your belief until after the wedding. At the reception. We danced together. And you made a comment about hoping to be a good father."

Her words came faster now.

"I was horrified. But your vows had already been spoken. The ceremony had taken place. It was the most awkward moment of my life. I considered telling you then. But, instead, I asked you if you loved her. And you said yes. So...I kept the truth to myself."

"What was I supposed to have said?" he asked

softly. "I thought she was going to have my baby. I'd decided to try to make it work."

The laugh that issued from him didn't have one iota of humor attached to it. "Honorable."

"What?" she whispered.

He sighed. "The guys thought my marrying Olivia was honorable. They also said I was stupid and gullible. And they were right." He picked up a pencil from the desktop. "So very right."

"Her conscience began to eat at her almost immediately," Rachel rushed to say.

He frowned. "Not until *after* she'd become pregnant with the girls, I'm sure."

Again, Rachel was unable to meet his gaze.

"She knew you were unhappy, Sloan. She had great respect for you. The way you went right out and found a job to support yourself and her and your new family. She told me that, once the babies came, you seemed so down. I told her that was natural for someone who had had his dreams stolen from him."

He swallowed a lump in his throat at the thought that Rachel had taken his side all those years ago. That she'd understood him so well even back then.

"She'd tried to argue that she had hoped to give you new dreams," Rachel said. "Different dreams. But she admitted that had been a mistake. And she did all she could by offering you her trust fund as soon as it became available to her."

"Olivia told me the money should go toward my tuition as an investment in our future," he said around the sour taste in his mouth. "I didn't want to take her money. We argued about it. She wanted me to think of it as our money, not hers." He whispered,

"An investment in the future? That money was nothing more than atonement. She was trying to make amends...she was trying to appease her guilty conscience."

"She *was* investing in the future," Rachel argued. "Her future. And yours. As well as the girls'. And Olivia *did* love you. She may have discovered a little late just what that meant. That instead of manipulating you, she should have been doing everything in her power to make you happy. To help you attain your goals. Achieve your highest dream. But she did learn that. In the end, she realized it."

He reclined against the seat back and studied Rachel's face. Anxiety was still there, he saw. As well as numerous other emotions he couldn't put a name to. There was something about this whole conversation that he didn't quite understand.

"Why?" he asked. "Why are you telling me all this? Why is it necessary that I know that I was duped by my wife? Why is it so important to you that I understand Olivia's motivations for what she did? Why don't you let me feel the anger that any normal person would feel after hearing such news?"

She didn't hesitate in answering. "Because of the things you said to me in the coffee shop that morning. You feel guilty for not loving Olivia like a husband should love his wife. And every day of your life is colored by the guilt you feel. Everything you experience is tainted by it. You need to be free of it, Sloan. And I thought that the only way for you to get beyond it would be to understand the truth. The whole truth."

"All the truth makes me feel," he told her honestly, "is bitter."

Moisture gathered in her eyes, making them glisten with the same petition that was in her voice as she said, "Please try to understand her, Sloan. Not for her sake. For *yours*. Replacing the guilt you feel with anger and resentment isn't going to help you. Anger isn't freeing." She blinked, and a single tear rolled slowly down her porcelain cheek. "But forgiveness is."

"You want me to forgive her?" Incredulity rolled over him until he thought he'd drown in it. He toyed with the pencil in his hands, slid both thumbs toward each other, then apart, over and over. Finally, the wood snapped in two. And something inside him snapped as well.

"I need to be alone, Rachel." And when she didn't move right away, he repeated, "I need to be alone."

When the door of his office closed behind her, Sloan tried to let his emotions loose. There was so much to comprehend. So much to deal with. He should be feeling a multitude of things right now.

But all he felt was numb. And breathtakingly sad.

Chapter Ten

Saturday morning dawned brisk but sunny. And as Rachel dried herself with a fluffy towel, she came to a decision. She was going to hand in her resignation.

Oh, she didn't plan to move away. She'd stay in Philadelphia. Her determination to remain in Sasha, Sydney and Sophie's lives would prevent her from leaving town. But she didn't have to torture herself, day in and day out, by working in such close proximity to Sloan.

She loved him. She couldn't hide from that fact any longer.

However, she could also no longer hide from the fact that nothing—*nothing*—would ever come of the feelings she had for him. The relationship she shared with him was professional. Often it was friendly. And lately, it had grown into a deep attraction. But he was plagued by the past. And that fact would prevent them from ever becoming lovers.

Lovers.

She shivered as the word sighed through her being. She wanted so desperately to be Sloan's lover. To spend her life with him. To share every day, every night with him. To be his partner. His wife.

And she'd wanted that for so long, she couldn't remember a time when she didn't want it. But to continue living like this…to continue to suffer every single day by working next to a man she loved but couldn't have simply wasn't healthy.

She had to disengage from him. She had to make a life for herself. Oh, she would probably never marry. No man could ever compare to Sloan. No man she'd ever dated had. That's why she'd stopped searching. She knew what she wanted. But she just couldn't have it.

It was time to realize that fact. Once and for all. And it was time to do what she could to transcend it.

Another job wouldn't be hard to find. She was good at what she did. There were plenty of doctors in this city who would be happy to have her manage their offices. She knew that.

Thinking of moving on, of taking a new job, of leaving behind all that was familiar in her professional life, was frightening. Rachel wiped the steam from the mirror and stared at her reflection. Who was she kidding? The fear that froze her insides into something resembling the icicles that hung from the eaves of her building had little to do with her career. It had everything to do with not seeing Sloan any more.

Not that she'd never see him. If she intended to

keep up with the girls, which she did, then surely she'd have to interact with him. But not every day. Not even every week. Maybe she'd see him once a month. Or once every other month. Six times a year. She could stand seeing him that often, couldn't she?

For the sake of the girls, she could.

But the real question was, could she survive seeing him that *seldom?*

She'd have to. That's all there was to it.

She ran the brush through her hair. So the decision was made. She'd hand in her resignation and find herself another job. It was the right thing to do.

Are you sure?

Doubt whispered through her head, coursed over every inch of her skin until she wanted to flinch from it.

Her grip on the hairbrush tightened. Yes, she was sure. Now all she had to do was tell Sloan. Informing Travis and Greg of her intentions would be difficult. But not nearly as hard as facing Sloan would be. Yet, she'd do it. And she'd do it today.

The phone rang. She wrapped the soft towel around her and went to pick the receiver of the bedside phone.

"The party is just four hours away and everything is completely falling apart."

Hearing Sloan's anxiety-ridden tone, she didn't know whether to smile…or cry. The girls always had a way of getting to him, and that made her want to smile. But the fact that she was considering isolating herself from him—not being so instantly available when he had these sorts of crises—made her eyes well up with tears.

She would not cry. The new path she was determined to take was for her own good. As well as Sloan's. If she wasn't around, he wouldn't feel attracted to her, and he would have no more reason to feel guilty. This was best for both of them. She had to remember that.

"It can't be as bad as all that." She kept her tone light in hopes of calming him.

"The girls have been in an uproar all morning," he told her. "Fighting over who's wearing what. At one point, both Sydney and Sasha were both wearing blue—not the same outfit, mind you, just the same color. And each was screeching at the other to change her clothes. I finally put my foot down and demanded they both change. No one could wear blue. In any shape or form."

He puffed out an exasperated breath that really did have Rachel smiling.

"It's been a nightmare. I haven't picked up the cake. The game room isn't decorated. I just pulled out all the ingredients for the sour-cream dip, but before I could get everything mixed the hospital called. Mrs. Lawrence is in the E.R."

"What's wrong with her?"

"The doctor on call says she's got a bit of congestion in her chest," he replied. "She's coughing. But that there was nothing to be concerned about."

"Can he write her a prescription for cough syrup?" Rachel asked. "Since it's not a real emergency—"

"She's asking for me. She's lonely. I just know it. She probably needs nothing more than someone to listen."

Rachel heard his resigned sigh and she knew he meant to travel to the hospital to see his patient.

"Can you come?"

"Of course I can," she told him. "I'll pick up the cake. I'll even mix up the dip."

"You'll have to get the girls moving on the decorations," he warned.

"I can handle it."

"There's no doubt in my mind," he whispered.

He was silent a moment, and the little hairs on the back of Rachel's neck stood on end as she wondered about the odd tone she had heard in his voice. But when he next spoke, the strange quality was gone.

"Can you come soon? I'll hurry on to the hospital. That way I'll get back here before the party. The girls will be okay until you arrive."

"It'll take me a few minutes to throw on some clothes," she said. "Then I'll be on my way."

When she let herself into Sloan's house, she was balancing the cake in one hand, a bag filled with presents in the other. Her ring of keys dropped to the floor, and she thought that she'd have to remember to return his house key. If she was going to distance herself from him, it would be necessary to take care of the small details.

A chill raked up her spine as she set the cake on the counter of the kitchen island, then the gifts. She'd experienced those same kinds of thoughts about Olivia so many years ago when she'd decided to move out of the apartment they had shared. She had never split rent or living space with her best friend again, but they had succeeded in repairing their relationship. Rachel knew that wasn't going to happen between herself and Sloan. The emotions he felt about the past were just too strong.

After rousing the girls from where they were fighting over the bathroom upstairs, Rachel hugged them all, wished them a happy birthday and assured them they looked fabulous. Then she ordered them down into the kitchen where she handed them rolls of crepe-paper streamers, scissors, cellophane tape, a tablecloth, matching napkins, plates, cups and a punch bowl and gave them instructions not to come up the stairs until the game room was decorated.

When they asked how they should decorate the room, Rachel had replied, "Use your imagination!"

They had shouted with delight to have been given such freedom.

While Rachel was mixing up the vegetable dip ingredients, the doorbell rang. She opened the door to find Greg, Jane and little Joy, as well as Diana, Travis, and his adopted Native American twins, Josh and Jared, standing on the front porch.

"We heard that Sloan had to go to the E.R.," Greg said.

"And we thought you could use a little help," Travis added.

"I could use a *lot* of help," Rachel said as she let everyone inside and several minutes were spent hanging up coats.

"Actually," Jane said with a laugh as she pulled off Joy's coat, "Diana and I came to help. Greg and Travis are going to play with the children." She handed the giggling little girl to her father.

"Come here, you." Greg smiled at his daughter. Joy patted his cheek and promptly pinched his nose.

"Ouch!" he said with a chuckle. Laughter bubbled from the toddler.

The three women went into the kitchen while the men stayed with the children in the living room. When sounds of a televised basketball game floated toward them, Rachel grinned at Diana's groan. "Travis said he didn't mind coming early as long as he didn't miss the game." She shook her dark head. "He bought the boys three new comic books each to keep them busy."

"Soon they'll be watching the games with him," Jane warned her. "You sure you want to marry into a house full of men?"

All three of them laughed at Diana's unhesitating, enthusiastic answer.

These women had come to mean a lot to her over the past few weeks, and Rachel considered telling them about her intention of resigning from her job. But she wanted to tell Sloan first. And she'd tell him at the same time she revealed her final secret about the past.

"Let's take some of the snacks downstairs," Rachel suggested. "And check to see how the girls are making out."

Jane and Diana automatically began gathering up the bags of potato chips, pretzels and popcorn that Sloan had bought for the party. They started down the carpeted steps.

"I think getting Dad and Rachel together—"

Frowning suddenly at Sydney's words, Rachel turned to her friends, pressing her index finger against her lips. The triplets' voices carried up the stairwell, clear as a bell.

"—has turned out just perfect."

Getting her and Sloan together? Rachel looked at Jane, knowing her expression silently conveyed her curiosity over what the child meant.

"Me, too," Sasha said.

Sophie quickly added, "Me, three."

Rachel knew Sasha's chuckle when she heard it. "That New Year's Eve gag has really freed us from Dad's tyranny," Sasha responded. "When they went out shopping together this week, I slipped over to Alice's house for a whole hour and Dad *never even knew it.*"

The utter glee in the child's tone shocked Rachel.

"And when they were up all night baking those cookies," Sophie chimed in, "I talked to Bobby on the phone *for hours*...until way past eleven."

"And they'd kill us," Sydney said, "if they ever found out we *volunteered* to bring all those cookies."

Stifling a gasp, Rachel stood frozen as the triplets' scheme slowly sank in. The girls had meant for her and Sloan to attend that party together. There had been no mix-up, no miscommunication. They'd *intended* for the two of them to become interested in each other. Those girls had *hoped* that her life and Sloan's would become mangled. They had deliberated. Calculated. All for the sake of finagling a little freedom from their father's attention.

Rachel thought of the heated kisses she and Sloan had shared, the secrets from the past they had felt compelled to reveal—and then, there was her decision to resign from her job. Surely, Sophie, Sydney and Sasha didn't have a clue how well they had succeeded in complicating two lives.

With a quick, pleading glance, Rachel silently requested that Jane and Diana remain out of sight for just a moment. She had a few things to say to the girls. The women nodded their understanding and then promptly sat down on the top two steps, obviously intent on not missing a thing that was said.

Rachel descended the stairs and entered the game room. "I cannot tell you how disappointed I am in the three of you."

Three pairs of eyes as big as saucers turned to face her.

"You should be ashamed of yourselves," she added. "And I think what hurts me most is knowing that you used me against your father."

Immediately, the surprise on all three of the girls' faces clouded with guilt.

"I've gone out of my way to do things for you," she said. "To take you shopping. To get your hair done. I've chauffeured you all over this city. I've helped you with your homework. And been a sounding board for your problems. As well as a barrier between you and your dad when you wanted to do things he'd rather you not do."

The expressions on their faces became bleaker and bleaker. But Rachel didn't let up. She needed to make them see how wrong they had been.

"And your father loves you," she continued. "All he's ever done is his best. His absolute best. To provide for you. To raise you up to be proper young ladies. To teach you right from wrong. And this is how you repay him. By manipulating him."

Evidently, Sydney could take it no longer. She said, "We never meant to hurt him."

"Or you," Sophie added softly.

"We only meant to..." Sasha obviously couldn't find the right words to describe their deed.

Rachel suggested, "Get away with something?"

In unison, the triplets lowered their chins in shame.

"I'm sorry," Sophie whispered.

Sasha added, "Me, too."

Sydney met Rachel's gaze. "I am, too, Rachel."

The fact that Sydney hadn't thought to use the habitual "me, three" told Rachel something. It revealed that the girls realized the seriousness of the matter.

Sasha asked, "Are you gonna tell Dad what we've done?"

"No," Rachel said. "I'm not. But the three of you will. I don't know how this will affect your party, but you've got to tell him. You've got to make this right. For your own good."

Sydney groaned. "Why do adults always say that?"

Rachel couldn't help but grin. "You won't understand until you're an adult with kids of your own." Once again, she grew serious. "I have one more thing to say. You thought that tossing me and your dad together would give you the chance to do whatever you want. Well, you're wrong there. As long as there's breath in my body, I'll be watching you."

From the stairwell, Jane called down, "Me, too."

"Me, three," Diana added.

Greg piped up, "Me, four!"

Then it was Travis's turn. "Me, Five."

The adults tromped down the steps, the little ones close on their heels, but the love beaming from each and every face told the girls that there was no anger to be found, only love.

All three of the triplets covered their faces and cried out.

"We're woefully outnumbered," one of them shouted.

"And don't you ever forget it," Rachel told them, laughing.

"It's not fair!" another yelled, giggling.

"What's not fair?"

Rachel turned to see Sloan standing in the doorway behind the group of adults, and her heart tripped against her ribs. My, how she loved this man. How was she ever going to tell him of her plans to leave his employ?

She'd do it. She wasn't sure how...just that she would.

"Are you girls in trouble again?" he asked his daughters.

"Just say, 'me, six,'" Greg prompted, his tone light, "and they'll know what they're *really* up against."

"Ah." Sloan grinned. "So it's the adults against the teenagers, is it?"

Everyone gave a boisterous nod.

"Me, six!" he stated emphatically and undeniably. "If I've learned anything it's that it takes a whole darn village to raise kids these days." He gazed at his friends. "I need everyone's help."

Rachel said, "I think the girls have learned today that you've got it."

She felt her knees grow weak when Sloan's dark gaze zeroed in on her.

"Can we talk a minute?" he asked.

"Sure." She started up the stairs after him.

He probably wanted to fill her in on what had happened at the hospital. Once he did, she'd tell the final secret. And then gently break the bad news about her resignation. She didn't want to hold it inside any longer than she had to.

Once they were in the kitchen, she asked, "How was Mrs. Lawrence?"

"As I thought," he told her. "She just needed an ear. She vented about her husband. About her son. About feeling lost and alone. I'd like to ask Diana to talk to her. Mrs. Lawrence is willing to set up visits with a counselor until she gets herself over this empty-nest hump. Will her insurance cover it?"

"I don't know. But I'll call first thing Monday morning and plead her case. She sure does need someone to talk to." Anxiety whipped and churned inside her. "Speaking of work…"

Words went hither and yon in her head, and she scrambled to gather them together.

"I want you to know," she began, "t-that I intend to hand in my resignation."

"But, why, Rachel?" He shook his head, clearly bewildered. "Why?"

The expression in his eyes startled her, and she got the distinct impression that she'd wounded him. She couldn't let this stop her. She had to plow ahead.

"B-because," she continued, then she faltered. Pausing only long enough to moisten her dry-as-dust lips, she inhaled deeply, determined to maintain her course. "There's one more…um, tiny thing about the past you need to know. I've told you everything else.

I want to tell it all. I *need* to. Get everything out into the open, plain and clear. And then I'll…I'll get myself out of your life.'' She hastily added, ''As much as I can, anyway. I hope you'll allow me to continue to see the girls.''

She wanted desperately to reach up and smooth the deep lines from his brow. But she didn't dare. Instead, she steeled herself and said, ''When I told you that I moved out of the apartment I shared with Olivia because of her plans t-to…to lie to you, that was only half the truth.''

Don't drop your gaze, she silently ordered herself. Chin up. This is the last time in your life you're ever going to have to go through this kind of humiliation. She needed to clear away all the fog in her head. And in her heart. Confessing this last secret to Sloan would do just that.

Locking her gaze on his, she said, ''I left because I w-was…I was terribly attracted to you all those years ago. I felt drawn to you, and I didn't want to do anything to hurt Olivia. She was my best friend. And I felt leaving would be for the best. For everyone. Olivia. You. And especially me.''

Now for the hardest part.

''And once I came back into Olivia's life,'' she continued. ''I realized that the attraction I felt was still there. And over the years…'' She closed her eyes, wondering if she could actually get her tongue to form the words. She could. She *would*. When she next spoke, her tone was a mere whisper. ''Over the years, that attraction has slowly grown into something deeper. Richer.'' She hesitated only a moment before adding, ''I've fallen in love with you.''

Thick emotion knotted in her throat, welled in her eyes.

"And that's why it's necessary for me to resign. I can't work with you anymore, Sloan. I just can't."

There was no need for her to explain further. He was certainly intelligent enough to figure out the pain she experienced, day in and day out.

The tiny smile tugging at the corners of his mouth baffled Rachel. What had she said that he'd found the least bit amusing? She felt hurt, the agony of thinking he might be laughing at her knifing through her.

"I brought you up here," he said, "to talk about something you said to me in the office the other day. That piece of advice you gave me about forgiveness being better for me than anger."

Rachel felt breathless, and wondered why he didn't comment on what she'd felt was a huge revelation. Had he not heard the things she'd said? Did he not care how deeply her feelings for him ran? Or that her love for him had been going on for so long?

"And I think you're right." He reached out and smoothed her hair back from her face. "I can't say that I've forgiven Olivia. That's something I've got to work on. But I can say that I'm not angry with her. How could I be? I mean, she may have lied and manipulated. But she didn't give me just one treasure. She gave me three. Those girls down there are the lights of my life. Being their father is the best part of my existence." Again, he reached out and caressed her face. Then he softly added, "Well, it's *one* of the best parts."

What was that twinkle in his eye? she wondered.

His smile turned to a full-fledged chuckle. Rachel swallowed, feeling as if she couldn't catch her breath, as if the world was spinning and spinning, out of control.

"I also wanted to see you alone to tell you something," he went on. "Something that's going to be much easier now...well, now that I know how you feel about me." His grin was like that of a self-confident schoolboy, large and magnanimous.

She blinked, her mind a jumble of thoughts as a torrent of emotions swirled inside her; anticipation, hope, longing.

"But before I reveal all," he said, "I want you to know that I've spent the last couple of days thinking. About Olivia. About her illness. And about you. About all the times you were there for me."

Rachel didn't think it possible, but his smile widened, his deep gratitude evident.

"You've shown me, more times than I can count, just how much you care about my girls. And in your concern for them, you also showed me how much you cared about me. I love you for that, Rachel. I do."

Had he really said those three little words?

He slid his arms around her waist, and when he pulled her to him, she didn't resist.

"That first night I kissed you...on New Year's Eve—"

"The girls had more to do with that than you can imagine." She'd finally found her tongue. "But that's their story to tell."

His dark head shook. "And it's probably a whopper, too."

She nodded, allowing herself to smile. "As you were saying…" she prompted.

He laughed, rich and full, and she placed her hand against his hard chest to feel the vibration of it.

"That's you all over, Rachel," he quipped. "Keeping me organized and on track." After a quick pause, he continued, "As I was saying, I kissed you, and it was as if someone had jerked the rug out from under my feet. I was overwhelmed by how desperately I wanted you. And all the things you said to me about Olivia, all the secrets you exposed…well, somehow you've chased away the guilt." He gazed at the ceiling for a moment. "Oh, I'll always be sad about her death. I'll always wish there was something more I could have done. But you did make me see that my not loving her didn't make her sick. And I did do everything humanly possible to save her life. As you said, we all did everything we could."

Gently, he lifted her arms and placed them around his neck, and she was eager to oblige. She slid her hands over his shoulders, laced her fingers at the back of his neck.

"So now it's our time," he whispered. "A time for happiness and fulfillment. A time for love. Don't you think?"

She spoke his name on a joyous sigh. "I've thought this for so long. I've dreamed of it. Hoped for it. *Yearned* for it. I love you so."

"And I love you."

As he said the words, as their lips met, she realized that there wasn't an inkling of guilt or hesitation to be found in her. And she sensed none in him. All she felt was love. And a heartfelt faith that their future together would be as bright and clean as new-fallen snow.

Epilogue

Fall had painted the city of Philadelphia with rich and vibrant hues. And Rachel had done her best to bring those colors inside the church for her wedding.

Standing in the receiving line, she basked in the love expressed in her husband's adoring eyes.

"I'm the luckiest man on the face of the earth," Sloan whispered into her ear.

Delicious shivers coursed down her spine.

"I've never seen a lovelier bride."

She smiled at his compliment. "And I've never seen a handsomer groom." Then she waggled her brows suggestively. "Or a sexier one, either."

He kissed her then, and joy seemed to swirl and dance about them.

Sophie, Sydney and Sasha charged at Sloan, their faces lit up with happy smiles as they hugged his waist. The girls looked beautiful in their wine-colored, floor-length dresses. The scalloped lace covering the satin fabric was dainty and feminine. But nothing was more stunning than the elated expressions on their faces. And when all that happiness was focused on Rachel, she knew she'd done the right thing in asking the triplets to act as her maids of honor.

"I don't think you've ever looked so pretty, Rachel," Sydney said.

"Me, too," Sasha added.

Sophie added, "Me, three."

The girls kissed her, hugged her tightly, and then took their places at the end of the receiving line.

The first of the guests to approach were Greg and Jane. Greg carried little Joy, who had become quite a little chatterbox with all the new words she was learning. Jane's gait was becoming more of a waddle as her pregnant belly protruded a little more each week. The Hamilton family would have a brand new member in two short months.

While Greg was busy clapping Sloan on the back, Jane pressed her hand to Rachel's cheek.

"I wish you a lifetime of happiness," the woman said.

Rachel's throat constricted with emotion. Jane had become a dear friend. "Thanks," was all Rachel trusted herself to say.

Next, Diana and Travis approached them, Josh and Jared trailing not far behind. The boys looked like little gentlemen in their proper three-piece suits and matching ties.

Travis and Diana had gotten married this past spring, and the ceremony had been utterly poignant. Diana's grandmother had traveled from the Kolheek reservation to bless the union. Rachel knew she would never forget the image of the elderly woman in all her Shaman regalia.

Diana had become a therapist in the practice, and her counseling skills continued to amaze everyone. She was proving to be a real asset.

"Your eyes are filled with bliss," Diana said.

Rachel hugged her friend. "That's exactly what I'm feeling."

Travis kissed Rachel's cheek, and then Josh and Jared shyly hugged both Rachel and Sloan before hurrying off to catch up with their parents.

Sloan gathered Rachel into his arms.

"I know I should be greeting guests," he told her. "But I've got this urge that I can't seem to conquer."

Before she could even speak, his mouth covered hers in a heated kiss. The wedding guests encouraged him with a cheer. The elation coursing through Rachel metamorphosed into a burning desire—a desire that would have to wait until later to be quenched. But that was all right. The eager anticipation of the passion they would share—tonight, and for the rest of their lives—was all part of the fun of this most blessed day.

With a possessive arm around her shoulders, Sloan gazed into her face. "I'm the luckiest man alive."

Rachel laughed. "If you keep repeating yourself, I'm going to start worrying about you."

Her husband's eyes glittered with love. "I can't help it. I'm only speaking the truth." Then he added, "I wish my parents were alive. They'd love you just as much as I do."

"Mine would feel the same about you," Rachel

told him, knowing the adoration that squeezed her heart was also shining in her eyes.

Then he glanced over at their close-knit group of friends. Greg and Jane were talking with Diana and Travis, their children darting in and out of the small circle they'd created. When little Joy looked as if she was about to teeter off balance, all three of Sloan's daughters ran to the toddler's aid. Joy squealed with delight at all the attention, and everyone ended up laughing at the children's antics.

"We may not have many blood relatives," Sloan said softly to Rachel. "But we sure have put together one hell of a family, don't you think?"

Realizing the truth in his words, Rachel nodded. "Our family is precious. Utterly precious."

*   *   *   *   *

In March 2001, look for
WHO WILL FATHER MY BABY?
Donna Clayton's
captivating new Silhouette Romance!

Big Daddy Brubaker is back!
And this time his heart is set on getting
his three bachelor nephews hitched—any
way he can! Who will the lucky ladies be?
Find out in...

THE BRUBAKER BRIDES

by
Carolyn Zane

**THE MILLIONAIRE'S
WAITRESS WIFE**
(SR #1482, November 2000)

**MONTANA'S FEISTY
COWGIRL**
(SR #1488, December 2000)

**TEX'S EXASPERATING
HEIRESS**
(SR #1494, January 2001)

Watch for these uproariously funny
and wonderfully romantic tales...
only from Silhouette Romance!

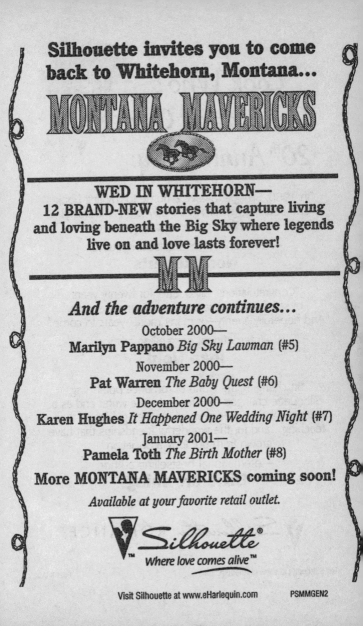

Look Who's Celebrating Our 20th Anniversary:

"In 1980, Silhouette gave a home to my first book and became my family. Happy 20th Anniversary! And may we celebrate twenty more."

—*New York Times* bestselling author
Nora Roberts

"Congratulations, Silhouette, for twenty years of satisfying, innovative, rich romance reading. And hopefully twenty—or many more—years to come."

—International bestselling author
Joan Hohl

"In changing the world of romance publishing, Silhouette changed my life, both as a writer and as a reader. I'll always be grateful for their guidance, their teaching…and for the wonderful friendships that have grown from our long association."

—International bestselling author
Dixie Browning

Silhouette ROMANCE™

Mature. Sophisticated. Experienced.
Complex. A bit cynical. Every woman's
dream man. Who else could it be but

Don't miss these stories from some of your
favorite authors at Silhouette Romance!

In January 2001 Arlene James brings you
THE MESMERIZING MR. CARLYLE
Silhouette Romance #1493
Rich, enigmatic Reese Carlyle had no business
pursuing Amber Presley. And then she learned
his secret....

In February 2001 look for Valerie Parv's
BOOTIES AND THE BEAST
Silhouette Romance #1501
A tiny baby, an irresistible woman...
has this gruff man met his match?

Available at your favorite retail outlet.

Where love comes alive™

#1 *New York Times* bestselling author

NORA ROBERTS

brings you more of the loyal and loving,
tempestuous and tantalizing Stanislaski family.

Coming in February 2001

The Stanislaski Sisters

Natasha and Rachel

Though raised in the Old World traditions of their
family, fiery Natasha Stanislaski and cool, classy
Rachel Stanislaski are ready for a *new* world of love....

And also available in February 2001 from
Silhouette Special Edition, the newest book in the
heartwarming Stanislaski saga

CONSIDERING KATE

Natasha and Spencer Kimball's daughter Kate turns her
back on old dreams and returns to her hometown, where
she finds the *man* of her dreams.

Available at your favorite retail outlet.

COMING NEXT MONTH